MW01110419

David Dillon

2/1/2024

#1

PROOF!

Dave Dillon

WELCOME TO PARIS

A light drizzle falls as Barry stares through the drops racing in a zigzag pattern down the small oval window. Behind him is the rustle and banging of luggage and clothes bags being removed from the overhead bins. "What is waiting for me here, I wonder?" Barry muses to himself. Soon, the conga line has departed and he gets up and grabs his grey, medium sized carry-on. He walks to the front of the plane and joins the last passengers straggling to get out the door like the last horses squeezing out of the coral. He can smell the rain as a breeze squeezes between the ramp covering and the open hatch.

"Merci," says the flight attendant, "welcome to Paris."

"Have a nice stay. Au revoir," says another.

Barry walks up the brightly lit corridor and into the gate terminal. Old men hobble along and women dragging lines of children scurry to and fro. Business people walk quickly from gate to gate trying to make their flights. A man with a deep voice blares in French over the loudspeakers. After a brief stop at the necessary, Barry finds himself in line at customs.

"Your passport, s'il vous plait," says the customs officer through a thick French accent. Once through customs, Barry walks into the main terminal. He has never been to Paris and his attention is distracted by the airport's marvelous architecture. As he enters into the terminal, there are two men standing near the opening as part of a

1

long line of people in anticipation of being greeters. Both of them have on rain slickers. One of them is holding two umbrellas and the other is holding a small cardboard sign bearing the name Dr. Barry Dowell in scrawled marker.

"It's not too late to turn back," Barry thinks to himself. "But I'm already here... What do I have to lose now?" Barry approaches the men and announces, "I'm Barry Dowell." The man holding the sign extends his hand and says with an accent much less than that of the customs officer, "Bonjour, Dr. Dowell." The other man hands one of the umbrellas to the man talking and reaches for Barry's carry-on.

"My name is Charles Dubois and this is Rene Dubois... and no, we are not related," the first man says rather drolly. He grabs hold of Barry's arm and starts to pull him towards the front doors. "The car is right this way, Dr. Dowell."

"You can just call me Barry."

The rain is still falling in a drizzle. More people scurry back and forth holding newspapers over their heads and trying not to step into the deeper puddles. Rene opens the trunk to a small blue sedan and throws Barry's bag in with little care and then slams the lid closed. Charles opens the back door and Barry climbs into the back seat. Both men close their umbrellas and get into the car. Soon Barry is being navigated through the streets of Paris as Charles and Rene argue as to the best way to go, speaking in French and pointing down different streets. The rain makes it difficult to see much and the usually bustling sidewalks are all but abandoned. Charles turns in his seat and asks, "So, Dr. Dowell, is this your first trip to Paris?"

"Call me Barry... Yes, yes it is," Barry replies while still staring out the window.

"I'm sorry the weather is not cooperating. So, you are from Texas?"

"Yes. My home is a little town called Wimberley, but right now, I'm living in Houston."

"I've always wanted to visit Texas. Do you own a lot of land there?"

"No," Barry chuckles, "I live in a little apartment, actually. So, what can you tell me about this job offer?"

Rene shoots a quick glance to Charles as Charles looks to Rene out of the corner of his eye. There is an uneasy silence. Finally Charles says hesitantly, "Actually, I have been instructed not to say anything, Dr. Dowell."

"Barry..." Barry interrupts.

"And really," Charles continues, "I don't think I could really explain it very well even if I could tell you. You'll just have to wait until we arrive."

"Can you at least tell me where we're going?" Barry inquires.

"Certainly. Our facility is just north of Troyes," Charles says as he turns back around.

"Oh... that helps," Barry mumbles to himself. They leave the confines of Paris and Barry goes back to looking out the window as Rene and Charles mumble in French and the small blue sedan races headlong into the grey countryside.

The car approaches a gate which leads into a fenced compound. A uniformed soldier waves them through. "I didn't know this was a military project," Barry says trying to glean a little more information.

"It is a civilian project," says Charles. "But we do have some military on loan to us for security. Nothing to be alarmed about."

"If there is nothing to be alarmed about," asks Barry, "then why do you need such tight security?" The question is ignored as the car drives between some very vanilla-looking, drab blue buildings set into a very rigid grid pattern. Once past the buildings, Barry can see a small opening into the side of a small hill. As the car drives toward the opening, Barry asks in an excited boyish voice, "Are we going underground?"

"Yes," replies Charles, "Most of the complex is underground."

"How far down does it go?" Barry asks.

Charles and Rene chuckle. "You watch too many movies, Dr. Dowell. There is only one level. We have it underground because some parts of the project have very rigid temperature constraints. It's easier to maintain a constant temperature this way."

"Oh," Barry sighs sounding somewhat disappointed.

A conventional looking security guard stands just in the opening. Once inside, the car pulls into a parking space and Rene and Charles jump out of the car. Charles opens the back door as Barry is reaching for the handle. Barry climbs out of the back seat and raises his arms to stretch. He sees Rene heading away with his bag. "Where is he going with my bag?" asks Barry.

"He is taking it to your room. I've been asked to escort you to the meeting room as soon as we arrived, this way, please," says Charles as he motions towards a door leading into the complex. Barry is walking down a hallway not unlike any hallway inside any office building. The walls are mostly bare, the colors are neutral and it has a very sterile, military feel about it. Charles stops at a door and opens it. He steps back and motions Barry through the door.

"If you will wait here, Dr. McDonald will be with you shortly." Barry walks through the door, which is shut behind him, into a very standard looking conference room. There are a dozen high-backed, plush chairs around a long table. The table contains a conference style phone and network cables come up though a hole in the center and lay strewn about on the tabletop like tree roots. There is a projector screen on the wall at one end and a projector mounted from the ceiling. A series of large windows make up the upper part of the wall that contains the door. Barry walks slowly over to one of the chairs and sits down. He stares across the table and out the windows watching people race back and forth in the hallway as they go about their business. After a few minutes, the door opens and two men enter. One is a large man with a red goatee carrying a pile of papers and the other is a tall lanky man carrying a laptop. The large man sets the papers down on the table and extends his hand.

"I'm Dr. Steven McDonald. I'm the one who called you," he says with an accent that sounds very Gaelic. "How are you?"

Barry responds as they shake hands, "I'm good."

"This is Dr. Edmond Bonnet," Steven says as he motions to the second man who is already sitting down and grabbing a network cable to plug in his laptop. "Sit down, please. Can I get you anything, Dr. Dowell? Something to drink?"

"Call me Barry, please. No, I'm fine right now." Barry says as the two sit.

"Sorry for all the James Bond stuff. I'm sure you're ready to know why you've come here."

"Yes," Barry says with a sigh. "That would be nice."

"Yes… Well…" Steven continues, "This is a very secretive project and before I can tell you anything, you must sign some paperwork."

"Paperwork?"

"Just some non-disclosure agreements… security verification forms… stuff like that," Steven says as he parses up the paper stack into small piles. Barry signs paper after paper, form after form as Steven throws them in front of him with a quick summary of what each document contains. After Barry is done signing, Steven assembles them into another master pile and slides them to the end of the table. The projector comes on and Edmond's laptop is displayed on the screen. It starts to download files and suddenly it shows a logo with the letters: P, C, E and D.

"Ok," says Steven. "What I'm about to tell you is very top secret. You've already signed to the fact that nothing leaves this compound and, if you do tell anything to anybody before we're done, you'll be sued by several countries – not to mention numerous companies and individuals. Our project here is Proof of Christ's Existence and Divinity."

"Not a very catchy title," Barry remarks.

"Well, we didn't have any money left over for marketing. Do you like science fiction shows, Barry?" Steven asks in a hypothetical tone.

"Which shows?"

"The ones where people travel from one place to another… through 'wormholes' in the fabric of space."

"Yeah, I've watched a couple of them."

"About fifteen years ago, there was a secret experiment conducted by the French government here involving nuclear stuff. It's complicated. But instead of achieving what they had set out to do, they accidentally stumbled across one of these wormholes. Here, in this mountain."

"What?" Barry says in a skeptical tone. "You dragged me to France to tell me you guys can go to another planet. What does this have to do with me?"

"No one said another planet, Dr. Dowell," Edmond says in a condescending voice.

"We think it actually goes back into the past," says Steven.

"Think? You guys have no idea where this thing goes?" Barry exclaims.

"Barry, as I said, they came upon it by accident. Forget what you've seen on TV. The truth is, it's been fifteen years and we're still guessing at things. I was not on the project at the time. But the government project was then changed to see if it could be opened again. It took about five years to get to a point where it could be opened on demand. It takes so much energy to maintain, we can only keep it open for seven to ten minutes. Any longer than that and lights around this entire region start blinking out."

Barry leans back in his chair. "Wow. But I still don't understand why I'm here?"

"Stick with me," Steven continues. "Once we could stabilize the opening, we sent probes in to see if we could get back data. Edmond…" Steven points to the screen and Edmond brings up a picture of a night sky. "This is a picture we were able to get back of the sky," Steven says turning back to Barry. "It's Earth because the constellations are the same, but they are not in the correct alignment." Edmond clicks his mouse a few times and another picture overlays the first one on the screen. "This is where those stars are today with the lines representing the key star movement. We calculated that this picture sent back was taken about the time of Christ, about twenty to thirty A.D. Both pictures were matched up using landmarks that were also photographed. Both pictures were taken in the north-eastern corner of the Sinai Peninsula."

"I think I could use a drink now," Barry says in a mesmerized voice.

"Coke?"

"Yeah. That's fine… if you don't have anything stronger."

Steven punches some buttons on the phone. "Traci, will you bring us a Coke and a Dr. Pepper?"

"Right away," the phone chirps.

"I have Dr. Pepper imported from the states. I got hooked on it several years ago when I was in Louisiana."

"So what else do you have besides pictures?" asks Barry.

"I'm afraid not much. Since we can only open the port for a short time, when we have the opportunity to go back, the equipment is sometimes malfunctioning for some reason or it's unreachable. We're not one hundred percent sure why."

"So, everything you send through is destroyed…" Barry formulates.

"We didn't say that!" Edmund snaps in a gruff French accent. "It's just sometimes unresponsive. The only way we can know for sure is to send a team through who can communicate from the other side once the port is re-opened."

"Ok," Barry sighs. "Let's get back to this Christ angle. Do you actually intend to contact Jesus Christ through this thing?" Barry asks in a lighthearted tone.

"That is precisely what we intend to do!" quips Edmund smugly.

"Well, not really contact," Steven interrupts, "more like observe. We want to go back and observe the culture, the people and yes, Jesus Christ… if that's possible… and document his ministry. That is where you come in."

"Me?" Barry says stunned.

Steven says something to Edmund in French and the presentation pops away and is replaced by an image of Barry's resume. "You are Dr. Barry Dowell? Ph.D. in Religious Studies, Judaism from Northwestern University… Author of 'Christian Roots In Judaism'… Has shown a propensity to take risks and challenge the status quo."

"Wait, wait, wait… I'm a little fish. There are bigger names than me out there." Barry argues.

"And what we are about to attempt is dangerous. I won't lie to you. You are young with no ties. No wife or children. We need someone who is un-tethered on the other side who knows what they're talking about."

"You mean someone who is expendable. Someone that the world won't miss if they disappear."

After some hesitation, Steven shakes his head and in a grim voice says, "Yes. I guess that is what I'm saying. You will be taking a great risk to make a great profit."

Barry chuckles, "Ha! I'm certainly no prophet!"

"No, no!" Steven replies. "A great profit - as in wealth and fame type profit. If you pull this off, you'll be able to change history."

"Yeah, like anybody's going to believe whatever I bring back. I'm not sure I believe all this stuff yet. It's all crazy!" Barry retorts.

"It is all a little overwhelming at first…" explains Steven

"A little?" Barry interrupts. "You bump into this wormhole-thingy that you think goes back to the time of Christ. So you're just going to jump through and take a casual look around, snap a few 'pics' of Jesus – if you can find him, because most everything we know about that timeframe is an educated guess at best – and then pop back. That's based on the assumption that you won't die ten seconds into the mission because everything you have sent through so far has stopped working! Does that about cover it?"

"Yep…. That about covers it," Steven replies.

After a few moments, Barry says, "I need to think on this."

"Of course," says Steven. "You have until tomorrow morning. Then I will need an answer." Then after a short pause, "Why don't I show you around the facility. Come this way," Steven says as he motions to the conference room door. They exit the room and leave Edmund disconnecting his laptop.

They begin to enter the lab areas. There are lots of computers and machines whirring with blinking lights and people scurrying to and fro with white lab coats and clipboards. "How did you fund all of this without anybody finding out?" asks Barry.

"Well, I wouldn't say 'Nobody' knows about it. This project was first funded by the government of France, but as it got bigger, other governments stepped in," explains Steven. "Once we theorized that we could go back to the time of Christ, and not to another galaxy, we had a couple of religious denominations and organizations chip in funding as well."

"Which ones?"

"Well, I can't say. Honestly, I don't know myself. Most of our funding is anonymous. Some think they will gain religiously while others hope to capitalize on the information commercially. Then there is our deal with a couple Hollywood and television studios."

"Hollywood?"

"Of course," Steven smirks. "Did you think they came up with this whole wormhole plot concept on their own?"

Barry chuckles, "And so what is our cut in this? How much do I make if I say yes?"

Steven stops and contemplates for a moment as Barry stands next to him awaiting the answer. "Well, you see…. There in is the rub, as they say."

"What do you mean?" Barry asks confused.

"We…," Steven says as he points around to several people scurrying by, "don't really get paid anything for the work we're doing." Barry frowns with a perplexed look.

Steven continues, "You, as the 'theological team member' will have exclusive rights to whatever it is we... that is... you discover."

"I'm still not following..." Barry laments.

"Ok, for the sake of argument, let's say you go there and get proof of Christ's miraculous healings. And then, you bring that proof back."

"Ok..." says Barry.

"So, let me ask you, what is the most popular, most sold book in the entire world?" asks Steven.

"Simple, it's the Bible." Barry answers.

A small boy-like grin runs across Steven's face. "What if the book of your findings were number two?"

Steven turns to walk away as the same boyish grin appears on Barry's face. He begins to almost robotically follow Steven and the only words he can muster are, "Oh, my..." Barry's mind starts to whir with thoughts of fame and fortune,

The two approach a small area off in a corner. A very military looking man sits in a small, wheeled, wooden chair at a desk filling out forms. "Jean-Louis," Steven calls out. The man swivels around in the chair. He looked like a soldier who had seen his due. "This is Dr. Barry Dowell." The man stands to shake Barry's hand. Steven continues as he motions to the man, "This is Jean-Louis LeVerrier. He is on the team and what you would call... our pilot."

"Bonjour," says Jean-Louis and the men shake hands. Just then, a man in a white lab coat and glasses, carrying a clip board, walks up to Steven and says something in French in a frantic manner. Steven looks away to where the man is pointing and then looks back to the clip board. After a brief conversation, the man scurries off. Steven says, "There is a problem I need to attend to. Why don't you sit here for a 'sec' and get to know Jean-Louis." He then says something to Jean-Louis in French and then turns to frantically follow after the man that left. Jean-Louis chuckles and tries to hide it by wiping his hand across his mouth.

"What did he say?" asks Barry.

"Sit down," says Jean-Louis as he rolls back to the desk and grabs an armless, wheeled chair. He rolls it to Barry with his foot in a kicking motion. "It seems Steven wants me to 'baby sit' you for a moment and try to convince you to join the team."

"Ah," says Barry, as he turns the chair around backwards and sits straddling the seat with his arms on the back. "LeVerrier... I seem to remember hearing that name in my college days."

Jean-Louis leans back in his chair and says, "My great-grandfather was French astronomer, Urbain Jean Joseph LeVerrier. Jean comes from him, Louis is from my father. Urbain had something to do with helping find the planet Neptune. He also had something to do with weather predicting, I think. To tell you the truth, I should probably know more about him, but my dad told the most boring stories when I was a kid." A small smile broke onto Jean-Louis's face.

"Is that how you got mixed up in this? So, what's your story?" Barry asks and then adds quickly, "Since your baby sitting..."

"No... I was a pilot in Armée de l'Air... The French air force. Until a training accident grounded me. I didn't want to be, how you say, 'desk jockey'?" says Jean-Louis.

Barry nods his head, "Yeah..."

Jean-Louis continues in a melancholy tone, "So, I found a chance to serve my country and still be a pilot. But I don't know why they call me a pilot... the machine almost flies itself. At least in theory."

"The machine?" Barry inquires?

"That's what I call it. So, what about you? You're the one they picked to replace Boris?"

"Wait… Replace?" Barry asks in a panicked tone.

"Oh, they haven't gotten that far I guess. Boris was the religious guy who was on the team. Last week, de l'appendicite exploded." Jean-Louis makes an exploding motion with his hands and voices a small exploding noise.

"What blew up?" Barry asks with raised eyebrows

" Oh… ah…" Jean-Louis says searching for the word. "Appendix?" he says pointing to that area on his body.

"Oh! Right," Barry says and heaves a little sigh of relief.

"Not that it was a bad thing – I never really liked him anyway. A fat Russian…. Big ego… Talked too much."

Steven reappears towards the end of the conversation wearing a white lab coat. "Yeah, guess you were telling him about Boris…"

"Oui. He has not seen the machine?" asks Jean-Louis as Barry spins around in his chair.

Steven says with a semi-disgusted tone, "Team Personnel Transportation Capsule."

"Woo, they had marketing money for that," Barry loudly whispers to Jean-Louis. A perplexed look leaps onto Jean-Louis's face as Steven heaves a heavy sigh. Barry adds, "Never mind."

"Why don't we go look at the capsule now?" Steven says in an exasperated voice and motions with his hand towards the other side of the room.

"Au revoir," Barry says to Jean-Louis as he gets out of the chair. "Glad we had this chat."

"Me also," replies Jean-Louis.

"So, I'm the replacement?" Barry asks as he and Steven head towards a doorway and more halls.

"Yes. I was going to get to that. I'm assuming Jean-Louis told you the whole story."

"I think so."

"So, you can see with the launch date less than three weeks away…"

"Whoa! He didn't tell me that part…" Barry interrupts.

"That is why you have until tomorrow morning to give me your answer," Steven continues. "After that I have to move to the next candidate – I'm running out of time very quickly."

"So you just didn't pick me because of me. I'm just one on the list."

Steven stops walking and turns to face Barry. "Ok, you want the big picture? I'll put it all out on the line for you," he says in a very serious tone. "I put your chances of surviving this at about fifty-fifty. If you do, you'll be one of the most famous and richest men in history. If you don't… well, then you don't. You're right. You aren't the *only* one on the list. But you were the *first* one on the list. But if you're already going to back out, now is the time. Before you see any more. Because, I'll find somebody on that list to go."

Barry looks down at the floor for a few moments thinking and there is an awkward silence. He then looks back to Steven and says, "Most famous in history… Ok. Let's see the whole enchilada."

Steven turns and walks a few doors down and slides a card through a reader mounted on the wall. "Ok," says Steven. "This is it."

He opens the door and the pair step through. It is a large, dimly lit room and there is a loud hum of computers and air rushing past his face. In the center of the room is a capsule lit in bright lights that looks like a cross between a jet fighter cockpit and a carnival ride bolted to a frame.

There are computers everywhere and cables hang down in several areas like black, motionless waterfalls cascading to the floor. Once on the floor, they run like spaghetti as they crisscross under a series of elevated walkways. There are some people scattered into several groups engaging in conversations and occasionally moving about as groups. There is not much light in the room and most of it is focus on the capsule. It all looks like a movie set out of a dream. Barry just stands motionless taking it all in. In front and in back of the capsule are large, steel structures that look like partial geo-domes opening towards the capsule. It almost looks like a big catcher's glove on both sides. There is a slow, deep, pulsing hum emanating from around the capsule. For the first time since he arrived, the impossible begins to take on an air of possibility. What seems like a farfetched tale begins to take shape into a real concept as the darkness closes around Barry. He feels, for the first time, that a greater power is moving in him and a strange sense of purpose now takes hold of him. After what seems like a very long time in Barry's mind, he says in a very slow, mechanical voice, "You're starting to make me a believer."

"Good," Steven replies. "Well, we're in the way here and you need to meet the third member of the team. Let's go." Steven turns to leave and Barry is still motionless. He grabs Barry's arm, "Let's go."

"Ok," Barry says slowly, still in a kind of awe, and his head turns back for one last glimpse as he leaves the room. Barry is now lost in thought as he tracks behind Steven. In no time at all they pass through a door and are outside once again. It's dusk. The rain has stopped for the moment but there are still large puddles as they walk to one of the buildings Barry drove by earlier. They enter the building, which once again looks like a normal office building. They reach a door and Steven raps a couple of times on the door and then opens it. Barry follows Steven through the door and is starting to focus again. This is a medium sized office. Behind the desk across from the door sits a small oriental man. He could be described as chubby and about fifty years old. He has a small, round head and wears a pair of wire frame glasses that seem to meld into his face.

"Scotty, this is Dr. Barry Dowell," Steven says. He motions towards the small man who rises from the chair and says, "This is Scotty Wang. Of course, Scotty isn't his first name, but I've never been able to say his first name and I'm not going to try now!"

Scotty laughs as he leans over the desk to shake Barry's hand. "Won't you be seated, Dr. Dowell?" he says.

"Barry, please," Barry says as he pulls up a chair.

"Ok, I have one more task to do. I'll leave you two to talk," says Steven as he hastily exits the office and closes the door.

"So, you are replacing Boris?" Scotty starts off the conversation.

"Still thinking about it," replies Barry in a hesitant voice.

"I understand. It took me a while to make up my mind. Unfortunately, you don't have that luxury. Tea?"

"No thanks, I'm fine. Sorry, I don't mean to sound rude, but I didn't expect anyone oriental to be part of the team. Are you also a Christian theologian?"

Scotty laughs, "No offense taken. I am Buddhist, I'm afraid. I am an archeologist. I am on the team to bring back articles to be dated and cataloged."

"Oh, that makes sense now. I'm sorry."

"No apologies necessary. My interest in this adventure is purely scientific, not religious. In fact, I often laugh as few of the people on this project are strongly religious."

"Really?" Barry says startled.

"Oh, yes," Scotty continues, "I know that Jean-Louis is Catholic, but not strongly so... Steven claims he's... Anglican? Isn't that what the Church of England is? Yes... I'm sure that is what he claims. But as scientists, I think God takes a back seat around here most of the time."

"Ok, I have to say one more thing. Your English is incredible. I have several Asian friends back home and you barely have an accent at all. Where are you from originally?"

Scotty laughs once more. "I was born just outside of Beijing, China. I went to the university there in Beijing to do my undergraduate work. But then I studied for six years in London and finished my doctorate in New York. I then returned to London where I worked until I came here two years ago. My specialty is really Chinese artifacts, but for this trip, pottery is pottery. We'll do most of the work when we return."

"Wow. Sounds like you've lived quite a life."

"Yes, I've done about everything I've wanted to do... except get rich and famous. That is why I volunteered for this. If I'm going to go out, it might as well be with a bang!"

Barry laughed, "I hadn't quite thought of it that way."

"It's late. Have you had dinner?" asks Scotty.

"No."

"Let's go eat in the cafe in the next building while we talk. It's much better than the one over in the 'Bat-Cave'," Scotty says with a grin.

"Is that what you call it?"

"No," continues Scotty as he grabs his coat and motions Barry towards the door. "That's what Steven started calling it. It has to do with your American movie, Batman, correct?"

"Yeah," Barry snickers as Scotty turns off the lights and closes the door.

IN OR OUT?

Barry didn't eat much at diner and he is escorted to his room. It's not a bad room. It's about the size of a college dormitory room although it has a very military feel to it. It has its own bathroom with a Venetian folding door. A small, shallow closet takes up one end of the room. He has a bed, a desk and a chair. His bags are setting on the chair and Barry is sitting on the bed. He sits and stares to nowhere in particular as his options roll over and over in his mind. He hasn't done anything in his life yet. He's gotten one book published, but he hasn't gotten to reap any benefits from that. He hasn't traveled like he told himself he would do. He hasn't had a chance to get serious with the two or three prospects he has picked out as the future Mrs. Dowell back home. And yet… who turns down the opportunity to be the most famous man in history? And maybe the richest? But he has to come back first and that is a crap shoot at this point. Finally, he asks himself what God would have him do. He gets off the bed and opens his bag. He pulls out his Bible and carries over to the bed. He drops it on the bed saying, "Lord, give me a sign!" He looks down and the Bible has flipped open to the book of Isaiah, chapter 41. And there in verse 13, Barry reads, "For

I am the Lord, your God, who takes hold of your right hand and says to you, 'Do not fear; I will help you.'" Barry closes the Bible and thinks to himself, "The Lord has smiled on me. I'm going to be famous... I know I am. I have this feeling that Bible scholars everywhere will know my name."

The thought that God was on his side is not enough to let Barry fall asleep. He tosses and turns and then lays there in the bed staring at the ceiling, dimly lit by the ribbon of light that was coming from the hallway underneath the door. He hears the footsteps of unknown strangers walking up and down the hallway. He can feel his own heart beating and it pounds out the anxiety that is rampant in Barry tonight. But soon, the rigors of the day finally take their toll and Barry drifts off to sleep.

The next morning Barry's body explodes upwards into a sitting position as someone bangs on the door to his room. He looks around the dimly lit room in a daze with his heart now racing. He can hear footsteps walking away down the hall. Soon he hears the muted thud of another door being banged on. He leaches at his blanket and tries to wrap his body as he stumbles to his feet in the chill of the room. He reaches out with his free hand and feels along the wall for a light switch. He flips the switch on and there is a dim flicker followed by a piercing white florescent light that instantly floods the room. Barry squints his eyes to avoid as much pain from the light as possible and pulls part of the cover up over his head to try and shade his face. He stumbles back to the desk and looks for his cell phone. "Six o'clock in the morning? Seriously?" he thinks to himself.

After a brief shower that was on the cold-side and a few inquires for directions, Barry finds himself back at the café for breakfast. He gets a cup of coffee and is perusing a shelf lined with various pastries when he notices that Scotty and Steven are sitting together at a table. He wanders over as Steven looks up. "Barry," Steven says in a tone that was too chipper for this early morning hour, "You're already up. I was going to let you sleep in a little."

"Someone banged my door so hard, I think I broke something jumping out of bed," Barry says as he slides into one of the empty chairs at the table.

"Oh, sorry about that," explains Steven. "There's still too much military carryover on this project to my liking."

"You look like crap. Didn't sleep well did you?" inquires Scotty with a smile.

"Thanks… and no, not as well as I would have liked," Barry replies as he begins to sip his coffee. After swallowing, he makes a half-hearted attempt to clear his throat. "But, I'm in. God knows why, but I'm on the team."

"Excellent!" Steven says as he slaps Barry on the arm. "I'll get an admin to take you over to personnel and get you started. There's a routine physical checkout, a few vaccinations, yadda yadda…" Steven voice trails off as he takes a drink from his cup. He then gets up and says to Scotty, "I need the revised lists by noon, don't forget." As he turns to walk away he says to Barry, "We'll talk. Welcome aboard."

Scotty wipes his face with his napkin and also gets up to leave. "Good fortune to us all," he says to Barry as he exits.

Barry whispers to himself, "I hope so…" and takes a bite of his pastry.

Soon, Barry is being lead around. Filling out papers, getting medical tests and shots, getting moved into a more permanent room. He then starts meeting with astronomers, linguist and other professionals that begin to bring him up to speed on the project. The days drift by and start to blur one into another as the late nights and endless meetings and studying start to take their toll. He takes a minimal amount of training in operating the capsule, how to be a backup to Jean-Louis is case of trouble. He has to spend some time with experts in Hebrew and Greek brushing up the little he remembers from his university days. He never gets enough to be conversational, but he hopes he has enough to pick out ideas if he's eavesdropping. His face begins to itch as he has to let his beard grow, but that soon goes away.

In typical fashion, Barry learns that the 'launch date' had already been changed twice. After he joins the team, it gets pushed three more times due to problems found and unanswered questions. Then, the time finally arrives. The team leaves the next day. Tension is high and many of the people are edgy. Barry isn't hungry the whole day, but knows he needs to eat something. He manages to down a hotdog and some fries. The doctor gives him a shot to knock him out so he can get some sleep.

The next morning, Barry is shaken awake. It is Jean-Louis. As Barry's head clears, Jean-Louis slaps him on the arm and says, "It's time to become famous." Barry gets to his feet as Jean-Louis heads for the door. Several hours later, Barry is strapped into the capsule in the seat behind Jean-Louis. Scotty sits behind him facing towards the back of the capsule. Barry sits staring into his hands – they are shaking, and he is trying to breathe deeply and relax. His thoughts wander as he hears teams of people running down checklists in his earpiece. It is in this room once again that a feeling of dread and of purpose comes over him at the same time in a swirling array of emotions. It would feel to Barry that he's exactly where he should be if it weren't for the warnings coming from every fiber of his being.

Steven's voice then comes on. "This is the biggest piece of machinery we've sent through. If you should contact any of the other previous equipment upon arrival, it should be no match for the capsule. Good luck, gentlemen!"

Jean-Louis mutters something in French and then announces, "Very reassuring... Here we go!"

The two dome structures start to glow. Barry is now seriously considering if he will be able to keep from soiling himself. His hands start to tremble more violently now. Suddenly the capsule is engulfed in blackness like Barry has never seen. It's not like air or space that is void of light, but more like an inky, liquid blackness. The light inside the capsule doesn't even create a glow beyond the glass. A voice comes through Barry's earpiece, "We are tracking you now, do you copy?"

"Oui!" is Jean-Louis's response.

"You're gaining speed. Can you confirm?"

"Six point four... point five," Jean-Louis says.

"Say again, you're break... again..." the voice on the earpiece sputters.

"Increase confirmed and climbing!" yells Jean-Louis.

"Still... must... too fast..." the voice sputters in and out as the communication goes silent.

"Come back.... Can't hear you!" Jean-Louis yells again.

"What's happening?" asks Barry in a panicked tone.

"For some reason we keep accelerating. We never saw this with the probes. I'm trying to..."

Jean-Louis's thought comes to an abrupt halt. The blackness disappears just as quickly as it had engulfed the capsule. They exit the other side. It is night, but there is a full moon and the blackness gives way to them traveling at what appears to be a high rate of speed only a few feet off the ground. Barry is trying to peer around the panels in front of him to see where they are going. After what is probably only a couple of seconds of eerie silence, Barry hears Jean-Louis say, "Oh merde!" A split second later the capsule slams into a rock face with a thunderous noise and the sound of twisting metal and the canopy glass shattering. Barry moves his arms to try and cover his head and face. The capsule spins to the side and hits the ground and goes tumbling in a random way, bouncing and spinning. Barry is totally disoriented and his head is pounding as the capsule comes to a stop on its left side. As Barry comes to his senses, he's not sure if he blacked out for a short period of time. Barry finally begins to regain his composure and starts to assess himself and the situation. He feels his face and head and then checks his hands. There is a little blood, but he's not bleeding badly; at least from his head. He doesn't feel any tremendous pain anywhere on his body so he fights to remove the harness from the seat and free himself. Barry tumbles out of the seat onto the ground. It's sand and it is cool to the touch so the sun must have set some hours ago. Barry is slow to get up as he tries to regain his balance and he says, "Hello?... Anybody?" He tries to dust the sand off himself and continues to call out, "Jean-Louis.... Scotty... Anybody..."

The moon casts an eerie glow as the sand extends from Barry in every direction like a motionless ocean, only disturbed by a few large groups of rocks poking up like silent sentinels here and there. There are small parts of the craft scattered everywhere, popping up out of the sand like strange plants trailing back to the group of rocks they hit. Barry stumbles around to the front of the capsule. "Jean-Louis?" Barry whispers with hopeful expectations as he peers around the front. Barry falls to his knees and begins to gag. The moon renders what is left of Jean-Louis in pale shades of blood and skin. Barry begins to cry as the horror begins to set in and shock takes hold of his body. The top, right half of Jean-Louis has been ripped away and what remains, dangles from the harness. Barry rolls onto his side as he continues to whimper. Random thoughts begin to flash through his mind as nothing is making sense anymore. At some point, Barry blacks out.

The moon is gone and the sun rises over the horizon to begin its climb into the sky. Barry struggles to open his eyes and holds his hand up to shield his face from the sun. The wind is picking up and starting to blow clouds of sand past his body and he can feel the grit on his skin. He begins to look around as the sun casts long shadows across the sand now. The light of day brings him no comfort as is makes even more gruesome the horrific death of Jean-Louis. Barry stands up and makes his way to the back of the capsule. It is almost completely stripped away. Barry scans the horizon and catches a glimpse of what looks like Scotty. Barry races over to the spot. It is Scotty. He's lying on his back in the sand and manages a small hand movement and whispers, "Barry...."

Barry kneels down next to him and says with great relief, "You're alive. Let me help you..."

"No!" Scotty commands with a sudden look of agony on his face and a pain-filled voice. "Don't move me. I think I broke my back. I think it's bad." The sunlight is creeping closer to where Scotty was laying.

"Hold on a sec," Barry said rising back to his feet. He looks around and sees a medium-sized panel sticking out of the sand. He retrieves the panel and brings it back to Scotty. Barry pushes the panel into the sand right next to Scotty's head and shoulder. "That will keep the sun off your face for a little while," Barry said as he walks to the other side of Scotty.

"Go out with a bang. Didn't I say that?" Scotty tries to laugh through a grimacing breath.

"We're not giving up yet." Barry tries to reassure Scotty.

"Where is Jean-Louis?" Scotty asks knowing what the answer will be. Barry says nothing. He can only close his eyes and shake his head. "Too bad," Scotty whispers.

"It's ok," Barry says as he clears his throat. "We just have to hold out until they re-open the portal. I'll find a way to get you back through."

"If it opens again," whispers Scotty. "Is there any water?"

"Oh, yeah," Barry says in hurried tone as he scrambles to his feet to try and find some supplies. He finds one of the food canisters partial buried in the sand. He opens it and finds some bottled water. "Hear, drink a little bit of this," Barry says as he twists open the top and pours a little into Scotty's mouth.

"A little more, please?" Scotty says after managing to swallow the water.

Barry asks, "What do you mean '*if*'? They said they can open it on demand after the power builds back up, right?"

"If it opens to the same place each time... this time. Part of the problem they had with probes was, when they opened the portal a second time, sometimes the probe would be gone. Or the two year battery would already be dead. What was discussed was that it was opening sometime within a three to four year window but not the same time. It was opening too early, before the probe had even arrived, or it was opening years after we sent the probe through."

"Did it ever hit the same time?"

"Hard to tell. The times we came back to a working probe could have been days or months or a year."

"Great!" Barry cries out.

"Guess they didn't mention that part, huh?"

"No," Barry says angrily as he stands up, "they failed to alert me to that little tidbit!" He kicks at the sand.

"The capsule has some kind of homing device. They hoped that once we were on this side, we could force it to open to the target each time. Jean-Louis was responsible for that part."

"We can't expect much help from him now. How can we tell if it's working?"

Scotty winces, "A little more water please." Barry pours another small amount into Scotty's mouth that he struggles to swallow. "I don't know. Like I said, Jean-Louis was responsible for that part."

"We can only hope it didn't suffer the same fate. Let me go take a look."

Barry walks to the capsule. As he stands there looking, the day is already heating up. He can see some lights flashing. He locates one light that is labeled as "Homing Indicator" that is flashing intermittently but not at a constant rate. It seems to flash randomly. Barry doesn't know if that's a good or bad sign. He walks back to Scotty and plops down into the sand.

"Well?" Scotty asks with reserved anticipation.

"It looks like a few things still have some power. I think the homing beacon is working, but I can't tell for sure," Barry whispers dejectedly.

It is mid-day and the sun beats down on the two men without mercy. Barry has collected more pieces and arranged them to keep Scotty's upper body and head shaded. He also musters the courage to pull what is left of Jean-Louis from the wreckage. He drags him a short distance and scoops out a shallow grave from the sand. He drags the body in and covers it up as best he can. Barry gathers up the supplies he can find and piles them into stacks near where Scotty is laying. He sits down in the shade next to Scotty's head. "We have enough supplies for a few days," Barry says as he wipes the sweat from his head.

"It won't be enough," Scotty whispers.

"Don't think like that! We'll make it. We're going to be famous."

"Take the supplies and leave me here. You have a chance of reaching a settlement or something."

"And what?" Barry asks slightly hysterically. "What if I do find a town? Do I ask them to call 9-1-1? Whip out my Visa card and check into a hotel?"

"You have to do something or we will both die here."

"Stop it. Ok? Just stop it. We're going to make it I tell you. God didn't lead me here for nothing."

Scotty manages to crack a small smile, "I hope so." He coughs a small cough and says, "More water please?"

It feels better now that the sun has set. The moon has once again taken its place in the sky and once again the area glows with an eerie tint. Barry stares up into the stars. He thinks of the fortune and prestige that awaits him if that stupid portal will only open.

"My mom, before she died," rambles Barry, "she said I was destined to be somebody. She believed that God had a special purpose for me. She believed that God showed it to her in a dream. At least, that's what she always told me."

"So you're parents were big Christians?" Scotty whispers

"Yeah. They dragged me to church every Sunday. My mom was the real believer. Sometimes I think my dad went just because my mom made him." Barry looks down and begins to run his finger through the sand. "Once she died, we quit going. Oh, we would go on Christmas or every once and a while… but once mom was gone, dad's heart just wasn't in it."

"But what about you?"

"I believe in God," Barry says as his gaze returns to the stars in the sky. "I went off to college soon after she died. It was probably because of her that I majored in religion. I knew I'd never make it as a preacher. There's no money in that. Maybe it was because of her I decided to come on this damn fool trip." Barry looks at Scotty and he's drifted off to sleep. Barry looks back to the sky. "Why did you let me do this?" Barry asks of God. "My mom said you had a purpose for me, why did you bring me here to die?"

STRIKING OUT

Three days pass with no sign of the portal opening. Scotty dies sometime during the second night. Barry awakes to find his body cold and without life. He buries him next to Jean-Louis. He now sits in the shade once occupied by Scotty and stares out to the horizons. The supplies are running low, having mostly been destroyed and scattered over the wreckage site. Most of the small pieces are now covered over by blowing sand. He has enough water for two more days if he's careful. The last morsels of food will probably disappear sometime today. Barry knows he has to do something. But his very being is numb. His mind wanders aimlessly through thoughts of his childhood, his life as it was and his life that could have been had he not made this decision. What options are left? He knows he has to go somewhere or die here. In the late afternoon, something inside Barry pops and, with renewed strength and determination, he decides that he will take off tonight. He does not know what he will find, but he is determined not to die here.

By dusk, Barry is ready to leave. He leaves a note for someone. Why and for whom, he doesn't have a clue. He checks to make sure his clothing is arranged correctly. He takes what few provisions are left, hides them inside his outer cloak and begins to walk away. After a small distance, he turns to look back. The shifting sand over the last few days begins to cover what remains. Would anybody find this wreckage? As this point, Barry doesn't care. He waves half-heartedly to his fellow travelers and whispers, "Rest in peace. Go with God." He turns and walks east. He doesn't know why he picks east. Perhaps it is because he remembers a spot on the map where they believed the portal was opening to. Perhaps it was just providence that chose the direction. Perhaps it was because he just didn't want the setting sun in his eyes. Regardless, Barry trudges on.

The moon was now beginning to swell into the sky. There is light, but all Barry can see are waves of dunes stretching as far as the light reaches. His feet slip and slide with every step as the sand gives way to his advance. As he climbs the dunes, the sand swallows his feet like hands reaching up and taking hold of him and making the progress difficult. But Barry presses on. As dawn approaches, the sun is rising to Barry's right. Somewhere in the night, providence turns his course north. With the rising of the sun, Barry sees an end to the dunes. He is able to see a rougher terrain in the far distance. It will take him hours to reach it and now he is a slave to the merciless sun. There is no shade here. It heats up the top sand quickly and now every step becomes more unbearable. But there is nowhere to hide. Barry knows he has to continue.

As the sun hangs high in the sky, Barry comes upon an outcropping of rocks that are arranged in a way that cast a small area of shade. He sits down and tries to cram himself into the small area afforded to him to escape the stare of the sun. The heat is still torturous, but it is better than it was. Barry decides to try and sleep here as best he can. As he drifts in and out of sleep, he can see his shadowy domain growing larger as the sun is forced to give up and can longer torture Barry on this day. He drifts back to sleep.

Barry awakens to find that the sun has set and night is upon him. The moon is waning as a small sliver erodes away ever so slightly each evening. But Barry knows that long before it reaches a new moon and will give no light, he will have to find food and water or he will be dead. He gets up and begins his trek anew. Soon the dunes give way to a flat but rocky plain. The earth is cracked and parched and his dragging feet kick up very little debris. Then in the distance the moonlight disappears and is replaced with a great, dark void. As Barry approaches, the void begins to take shape. He is on the edge of a great valley. Some parts of the valley floor are discernable far below him as the moon partially lights it. He walks up to the edge and kicks a small rock into the darkness. He hears the stone tumble and bang off other stones as it falls. He cannot tell how truly steep the cliff is, but he knows it is a long way down. Barry decides to carefully make his way along the edge. He is tired and finds a large bolder to rest against.

"Why me?" he continues to query God in his thoughts. He is beginning to grow delirious and he finds it hard to concentrate. "If you're going to kill me anyway, why don't you just get on with it?" He takes a small sip of his dwindling water supply. "Am I to be tortured as punishment? Please, just let me die." Barry can feel his strength failing and his mind weakening. He feels he cannot go much farther. He knows if he does not find food and water soon, this trip across the wilderness will have been for nothing. Once again, Barry drifts in and out of sleep. He pops awake as dawn is again approaching. He doesn't want to move, but forces himself to his feet and walks to the edge of the cliff. There is a large, rocky valley that stretches a great distance in front of him. At this scale, it seems devoid of any civilization. He can see a way down that looks negotiable. The relation of the cliff face to the sunrise will buy Barry some extra time before the sun finds him again. He decides to take advantage of that and begins navigating down into the valley. But he cannot outrun the sun, and soon it finds him again. Barry finds a large group of rocks that will suffice for shade for most of the day. He sits down and, for the first time since he left the wreckage site, he falls into a deep sleep.

Barry opens his eyes as the sun begins to shine in his face. He stands and stretches as he feels some of his strength returning. He estimates he has about three more hours of sunlight and another one or two of dusk. He begins to make his way across the valley floor. He reluctantly sips the last of his water. "Soon, my torture will end," Barry thinks to himself, "soon I'll be dead." And yet, something inside of him keeps pushing him onward. A will to live still flickers somewhere deep inside of him. The sun has set and the moon hangs on the edge of the valley, casting a small amount of light down to the bottom. Barry walks among the patchwork of a moonlit mosaic. Suddenly, Barry sees a dark mound on the ground. He cannot make out what it is at first, but it does not look like rocks. He slowly approaches until he is almost on top of it. It looks to be a man lying in the dirt as far as Barry can make out. "What do I do now?" Barry thinks. "Do I wake him up? He'll think I'm a bandit and kill me. Or he'll run off thinking I'm some kind of demon." But Barry can detect no movement at all; no breathing whatsoever. "Maybe he's dead," Barry thinks. Barry slowly approaches and shakes the stranger. There is no response, so Barry shakes him hard. There is still no response. Barry rolls him over and checks for breathing. He is dead. Barry is suddenly stuck with a thought. "Wait a minute," he thinks. "This is just what I needed. What a break." With a new energy that over takes him in an almost frenzy type manner, he begins to remove his clothes. "This guy is just about my size. I'll take his clothes. That way, if I do ever find someone, at least I won't look too out of place. I may even pass for 'normal'!" He starts to remove the stranger's clothes, remembering all the details of what goes where and how it's arranged. This unknown stranger didn't have much. Some undergarments, a dirty grey tunic, some sandals and a cloth girdle. Soon, he assumes this new identity, appearance wise at least. He drags the man over to a large group of rocks and stuffs him as best he can into the space between them. He takes his old clothes, which looks more like a Halloween costume in comparison to what he has now, and stuffs them under the dead man. "I told those guys to use real wool cloth and not that polyester crap," Barry says as he is stuffing his clothes away. He moves another rock up against the others as best he can so that it is as unnoticeable as possible. Barry then examines the ground using what light is now available and notices signs that look like the man dragged himself for a short time. Thoughts now race through Barry's head. "Which way do I go now? If I go the way he was headed, there is no guarantee that I'll find anything. What if he was stoned for a crime or something? If I go back the way he came, they might mistake me for him and kill me. Or they might think I robbed him and stole his clothes." After some debate, Barry decides to go in the direction his benefactor was heading when he died and hope that he knew where he was going. After a short while, Barry finds himself exhausted; all his adrenaline spent. He sits down against a rock and nods off to sleep.

Suddenly, Barry is awakened by a sound. He looks around but sees nothing. It sounded like the braying of a donkey. Then he hears it again. It is a donkey and it's coming from the other side of the hill in front of him. Barry races to the top of the small hill and stops dead in his tracks. There on the other side of the hill is an oasis. Barry had fallen asleep within one hundred yards of it. This is where his unknown benefactor must have been trying to get to. There is a small caravan of traders, who go unnoticed by Barry, on the other side of the oasis filling water jugs. Barry throws his hands in the air and shouts with joy. He races down the hill and into the water. He starts to scoop the water up in his hands and drink it. The men on the other side seem frozen in place as they stare at Barry. The water is gritty and warm, but water has never tasted better to Barry. After several gulps, he raises his hands in the air again and continues to whoop and dance around, splashing and sloshing the water. Barry then notices the other men. He stops and stands there in the water staring back, wet and dripping. One man begins to laugh and says something to the others. The men go back to filling their jugs and Barry exits the water. He now stands dripping on the water's edge and still staring at the men.

"Well," Barry muses to himself, "at least they're not trying to kill me. They're not even paying me much attention now. Maybe I can pass for 'normal'… as long as I don't open my mouth." Barry starts to wring out the water from his tunic. The men seem to be leaving as, one by one, the wagons and livestock begin to move away from the oasis. "Well, at least they didn't think I was demon possessed, I guess. I'm still stranded in the middle of nowhere, but at least I have water… and maybe some eatable plants."

One of the men shouts and Barry looks up. A man sitting in the last wagon motions to Barry and shouts something to him. It's not Greek and Barry doesn't understand it. All he can do is stand there and stare. The man looks at his friend in the wagon in front of his and the two exchange a few words. The man in the last wagon then shouts at Barry again and makes a 'come here' motion. Barry points to himself and the man nods his head and repeats the motion. Barry shuffles around the water to the other side and comes to a stop next to the wagon. The 'wagon man' says something else and points to the back of the wagon. "I think he's offering me a ride," Barry thinks. Barry walks to the back of the wagon. It is filled with some kind of flaxen or wheat and some barrels, but there is room for Barry to sit. So Barry hops up onto the back of the wagon and turns to look to see if that is what the 'wagon man' wanted. The 'wagon man' laughs again and says something to his friend and both of the wagons begin to move. "Not bad," muses Barry, "Not only have I passed as normal, I've also scored a ride to somewhere. To where – I have no idea…. But anywhere is better than nowhere." Barry leans up against the barrels and drifts off to sleep.

THE WAGON MAN

Barry is jolted awake. It is the 'wagon man' shaking him. As Barry looks down, he sees the 'wagon man' tearing at a big piece of bread. He hands a large piece to Barry and then grabs a clay cup from the edge of the wagon bed. He hands the cup to Barry and walks away. Barry looks into the cup and it's filled with water. He takes a sip of the water, which is warm but not nearly as gritty as the water he drank at the oasis. It is not until he takes a bite of the bread that he realizes that he hasn't eaten in days. He never thought bread could taste so good. He tries not to eat too fast, but it's difficult. What started as a large chunk of bread is quickly devoured. As the 'wagon man' returns to check on him, Barry swallows the last of the bread and burps and starts to gulp the water. The 'wagon man' looks Barry over slowly and looks surprised to see the bread gone already. Barry notices he's being watched and he freezes, looking at the 'wagon man' with that 'deer-in-the-headlights' look. The 'wagon man' laughs and gently tosses the piece of bread he is holding to Barry as he walks away again. Barry examines the piece of bread and it is obvious that it was the one the 'wagon man' was eating. But Barry decides he doesn't care and begins to finish off that piece as well. Although he takes a little more time eating this piece. He hops off the bed of the wagon to look around and to return some feeling to that part of his body which has been doing the sitting. They have stopped in a small village. There looks to be two dozen or so houses. There are things being taken out of wagons and other things being loaded on wagons. Barry tries to pick out a word or two, but they are probably speaking in Aramaic and Barry cannot glean the context. Not too far away is one of the men from this group talking to one of the villagers. He's stroking a donkey tied to a post. Barry thinks to himself, "I have no idea if he's selling that donkey, buying it, or just talking about the weather. I'm not hearing any Hebrew or Greek… I'm guessing it's Aramaic. I can't talk to anybody. What will happen to me now? Only God knows, but it seems that there's no going back now."

Some of the wagons are leaving and it appears others are preparing to leave. Barry hops back onto the wagon bed where he was. It isn't long until the 'wagon man' jumps on, gives Barry a quick glance and then urges his donkey onward. As they leave, several children follow them to the edge of the village. As the children stop, one waves at Barry. Without thinking, Barry waves back and the child smiles. He leans back against the barrels and relaxes. He stares off to the horizon and begins to think to himself. "So, now what? With each passing hour, I move further and further away from the portal. I have no money for supplies to head back there. And what would I find if I did get back? There is no guarantee that the portal will ever open to the time I'd be waiting in. It was so nice of them not to at least mention that little tidbit."

The wind picks up and some clouds start to roll in. Barry welcomes the shade, as does the 'wagon man' from what Barry can deduce. "There is no going back. I've got to face that now. I'm going to die in this forsaken place. Not exactly the riches and fame I had hoped for. What I wouldn't give to be back in San Antonio, along the river walk, sipping a little coffee and surfing the web." He shakes his head gently and lets out a big sigh.

One evening, near dusk, the 'wagon man' stops with the rest of the group next to a large body of water. Barry can't tell exactly how big it is in the waning light. The 'wagon man' motions to Barry as they all head for the water. The men wade into the water and start to wash off the dirt of the trip as they talk in what is idle conversation. Barry is given what appears to be a small rag to help in bathing. Once again, the others do not go out of their way to share anything but the minimum with Barry. That night at dinner, Barry sits off away from the others. He is given a small bit of meat, some bread and some water to drink. The others pass around some fruit and some wine as they laugh and tell stories around a small fire. It appears to Barry that they are willing to do what is necessary to keep him alive, but any charity beyond that does not seem to be required nor offered. Barry looks into the sky. Never before has he seen so many stars. Not even when he went on that backpacking trip to west Texas. A thought passes quickly through his mind and he whips his head around to look along the whole horizon. "Maybe I'll see the star of Bethlehem," he chuckles to himself. "Yeah, like I'd be that lucky." Soon the men quiet down and it appears to be bedtime for the group. Barry lies awake for a little while as he had slept until midday. Always pondering his fate and trying to figure out a way he could get home. Soon, the night finally does overtake him and Barry drifts off to sleep.

It has been twelve days on the road. Barry's back is stiff from leaning on the barrels. He periodically hops off the wagon and walks or jogs just to feel his body moving again.

The caravan is approaching a city. It is much bigger than the villages he had seen thus far. As the wagons roll into town, Barry gets more of a sense of home. The streets are wide, but split off in random directions. Some of them snake out of sight and others just seem to dead end. People are scurrying to and fro, paying no attention to Barry as he wheels by. There are women with various burdens of baskets and pottery who hurry in and out of doorways. There are men, some of whom are dragging small wagons or carts behind them, going about their work. "This is more like Houston," Barry thinks.

They pass an open market where lots of people stand talking and shouting. For a moment, Barry is caught up in the spectacle. These are the people he spent so much time studying, researching and theorizing about. And here they are in a '3D-live-action' reality playing out before his very eyes. In the market area, he is able to pick out some Greek, but it is different than the scholarly Greek he learned in school. The wagons pull to a stop and Barry hops off and begins to stare. He vaguely notices the 'wagon man' pass him and then Barry gets shoved from behind. Barry turns around and the 'wagon man' is pointing back down the road and mutters something in an aggravated tone. Before Barry can move, he is shoved again – more forcefully this time. The 'wagon man' seems to be waving him away down the road before turning to grab one of the barrels and moving it to the edge of the wagon bed. "Time to go," Barry thinks. "The trip ends here and now I'm in the way." Barry nods to 'wagon man' and then begins to walk back towards the open market.

As Barry wanders up the road, people continue to brush by him and walk around him with little or no regard. "I'm not getting any attention at all," Barry muses quietly. "I guess I do appear normal, at least appearance-wise." Barry wanders the streets for most of the day. Some spots are easy to pick out. He walks by a place where he can smell raw meat and assumes that is the butcher shop. He finds the well in the center of town where many people are hauling up water. He passes a place that appears to be a synagogue. He peeks through the doorway from the street and sees some benches but cannot see much more. He decides it might be best if he doesn't go in. Instead, he ends up sitting down to rest with his back to a wall opposite the synagogue. As Barry sits in the dirt resting, he watches the people go back and forth. "This is where I will die," Barry sighs. "I cannot communicate well enough to even tell them who I am. And if I could, what would I tell them?" He kicks at the dirt and whispers despairingly, "Maybe I could arrange for a book signing." The sun starts to set along with Barry's hope. As dark approaches, the streets become empty and Barry is left there, sitting in the dirt. The dark closing in is only surpassed by the depression in Barry's mind as all hope fades into an empty numbness. He cannot do anything except sit there and whimper as his strength drains away and he is left with the reality that he is marooned here. Lost in a sea of people who have no idea who he is or where he comes from.

Barry's hears something. He opens his eyes and the world is sideways. He fell asleep sometime during the night and is now on his side. He pulls himself into a sitting position once more. The sun has returned, although it's not shining directly on Barry yet, and people once more rush this way and that way attending to their lives among the long shadows and dim light. The sleep does not help Barry's mood. He is still depressed as he tries desperately to think of a way he can survive. He is lost in thought when he hears something fall to the ground. He looks up and a man pulling a cart has just passed him. Barry looks down and, near his feet; a coin lies in the dirt. Barry reaches across to pick up the coin. He holds it up and studies it. At first, he is fascinated by the coin itself as he looks at the details. But it is only a few seconds before the harsh reality bursts the bubble. "Well," Barry thinks with a deep sigh, "I think I've sunk as far as I can go. This makes it official… I'm the town charity case."

THE RAGGED BEGGAR

It has been about six months since Barry sat with his back to the wall that morning. After accepting that the town beggar is his official role, he moves across the street to a prime location outside the synagogue doorway. This allows the men entering the synagogue to give the beggar a token offering before they go make peace with God. Barry begins marking time with small scratches on a stone, but the uselessness of tracking days wears on Barry's mind and is eventually abandoned. Now Barry's day is fairly routine. He sits and collects coins during the day. At night, once the streets have emptied, he goes scavenging for anything he can find of use. Most nights he finds nothing of worth as people here do not throw things away. It is also the time when he can answer the call of nature in peace, go by the well to draw up some water to pour over himself to keep down the smell and walk around the town until he dries out. The money he makes buys a small portion of meat and some bread each afternoon. Barry manages to save enough to purchase a small blanket to cover himself and another old horse blanket he drapes over some sticks he finds that acts as a lean-to to shade him from the sun. The bad days are when it rains and everything gets soaked. It helps keep down the smell, but if it doesn't dry out before dark, it gets too cold to sleep. He also finds a small rusty metal box to put his coins in. He wiles away the days by thinking of plans whereby he can escape this nightmare, but none of his plans end happily.

Barry sits and waits for his benefactors to arrive. He knows them by sight now. He knows which ones throw him a coin every day, which ones only drop a coin once a week or so and which ones refuse to make eye contact with him. He remembers back to a little man who stood on the corner by the bookstore in Houston. He always wore one of three shirts and had on torn jeans in the winter and Bermuda shorts in the summer. He seemed to always have about three days of growth for a beard, never any more, never any less. He held a cardboard sign which Barry never bothered to read. He thinks about how many times he walked by that man and never made eye contact either. "I wonder now what his story was," Barry muses on several occasions. "Was he a victim of circumstances like me? Was he all alone, unable to communicate with anyone? Was he a con artist or just someone hoping to get a small piece of meat and some bread to make it through the day? Now I see those people every day… the ones that can't be bothered to look at me. I can feel the contempt they have for me without ever seeing their eyes. Is this how that old man felt every time I walked past him? I'll never have a chance to tell him how wrong I was and how sorry I feel now. Maybe this is my punishment for all of that. Maybe this is God getting even with me. Either way, it doesn't matter. God has forsaken me and I will live out the rest of my existence here."

One day, Barry strikes out a little earlier than usual. The rain has ended for the day and Barry wants to start drying out his garments before dark so he can get some sleep. As Barry wanders around the corner, he sees a man struggling with a large barrel as he tries to wrestle it down off a wagon. Without thinking about it, Barry runs up and grabs the barrel to steady it. Between the two of them, they manage to get the barrel down with only a minor thud as it lands on the road. Barry recognizes the man as one of his regular donors, although he only comes by once or twice a week. As Barry looks up, he notices the man's house. There is a fairly large courtyard surrounded by a short stone wall. Barry sees what looks like a forge in the back of the courtyard and a table with assorted tools. "This guy must be the town smithy," Barry thinks to himself. After examining the barrel, the man places his hand on Barry's shoulder and speaks something to him. Barry is surprised at the contact and jumps to face the man. The man repeats himself and Barry thinks, "I think he's saying 'thanks', but I have no idea how to say 'you're welcome'." So after a few seconds of awkward staring, Barry pats the man on the shoulder and turns to walk away. After a bit, Barry turns to look over his shoulder and the 'barrel man' is still staring with a perplexed look on his face. Barry chuckles to himself and continues on his way, determined to dry off before dark. He feels a small glimmer of goodness which makes his steps lighter today. It's the first time he's felt good about anything since he got here. It is a moment to relish while it lasts.

The next day, a pair of large feet walks in front of Barry and comes to a stop. Barry is surprised as nobody ever stops next to him. Barry looks up, shielding his eyes from the afternoon sun with his hand. Barry recognizes this person. It's the 'barrel man'. He is staring down at Barry and then squats down to look into Barry's face. Barry slowly lowers his hand and begins to stare back. The man says something to Barry, but he can't pick out any of the words. Barry just continues to stare. The man says something else, this time slower and drawn out. "This guy is actually trying to communicate with me?" Barry thinks. Barry shrugs his shoulders and shakes his head figuring the man will leave. But the man continues to stare at Barry and he can see the gears turning inside this man's head. Barry glances around to the people passing by. Evidently, this event is not enough to concern anyone else, as they continue to walk by and not notice. Finally the man points to himself and says "alone!"

"Alone?" Barry's brain is now awash with ideas as he intently looks at this man trying to figure out what he's saying. He points to himself again and repeats the word. "Is that his name? Alone?" Barry wonders. So Barry points to him and says, "Alone." The man's expression changes from a puzzled look to one of joy. He nods his head and with more passion points to himself and recites the word again. Barry gets caught up in the moment and laughs. Then the man points to Barry. "Oh, he wants to know my name. I'm not sure it will translate well, but we'll give it a shot." Barry points to himself and says in a slow manner says, "Bare-reeee." The man again gets a puzzled look on his face. But Barry points to himself and says his name again. The man points to Barry and repeats it. "Yes!" Barry screams in his head. "Somebody's finally paying attention to me!" Barry nods his head with a big smile.

The man stands up and says another word to Barry as he make a "come here" motion with his hand. It is the same word the 'wagon man' used at the oasis. "It must be the word for 'come'. He wants me to follow him," Barry thinks. "Ok. I'll play along and see what happens. After all, this is most exciting thing that has happened since I came here." Barry decides that nobody will steal his two moldy blankets so he leaves everything he owns behind. The man leads Barry up the street, all the time turning every few steps to say the word and make the motion. The fact the man keeps repeating the word to Barry as they walk, does cause some of the people they pass to do a double-take. But for the most part, the whole affair goes mostly ignored.

The man leads Barry to his home. It's the same place that Barry helped him with the barrel the day before. Waiting for them is an old man. "Who's the old man?" Barry wonders. "He's dressed like a rabbi… at least what I think a rabbi would look like." The 'rabbi man' and the 'barrel man' leading Barry talk briefly as they arrive. Barry figures the man must be a rabbi because he then comes over to Barry and looks him in the eye. He then starts chanting which is concluded by some hand waving and then he turns and leaves. Barry is still taking it all in and watching the rabbi walk away when the 'barrel man' tugs at his sleeve. Barry breaks from his trance and follows him over to a wagon. The 'barrel man' pats one of the barrels in the wagon and says another word to Barry. "So, what is that word?" Barry ponders. "Barrel? Water? Oil? What does he want?" The man repeats the word and so Barry says the word back. The man then makes the motion of moving the barrel using another word. "Oh, I get it," thinks Barry, "he wants help unloading. I guess he figured I was available since I was just sitting around. I guess he was right." Barry nods his head and makes the motion. He reaches for the barrel and it doesn't budge easily. "Dang! I can see why he needs help. This sucker is going to be heavy."

After several minutes, the two of them manage to wrestle the barrel to the ground with a soft thud as before. The 'barrel man' starts to tip it up on edge and Barry grabs the other side and helps. The two of them then roll the barrel on the edge into a store place. "I better get at least two or three coins for this!" Barry thinks as they roll the barrel. Once it's in place, Barry figures his job is done. But the 'barrel man' coaxes him back out to the wagon and loads his arms up with branches and wood. Several trips later, the wagon is finally empty. Barry is ready to get a couple of coins and make it to the market to get an extra portion of meat before it closes. But the man begins him on another job, all the time repeating a new word to Barry. By now, Barry has forgotten half of the words, but there is a strange warming of his heart as he finally feels useful. So he continues to do whatever the man wants him to do and the end of one chore leads to the beginning of the next.

It's getting close to dusk and now Barry is growing impatient. He has to leave soon if he is to buy food for the day and all this work has made him extra hungry. To make matters worse, Barry can smell the food being prepared inside the house and it is making him anxious. Finally the man comes and stops Barry from doing any further work. "Finally," Barry muses to himself, "now I can get paid and go eat... if they're not already closed." But, instead of paying him, the 'barrel man' leads him to the back of the house where he washes his hands and motions for Barry to do likewise. Barry begins to wash and he is given some kind of soap. He washes his hands and then his arms. It feels so good to finally be clean. He begins to wash his face and the 'barrel man' laughs. Before Barry can get too carried away, the 'barrel man' stops him and says, "Come." The man then goes to the doorway and steps into the house. He motions Barry inside. "What? He wants me to come inside? Does he plan to feed me for all this work? How lucky can I get?" Barry's thoughts now race. Barry hesitates, but the man is insistent and reaches to pull him inside several times. Barry steps in and follows the man to the far end.

The house has two stories, like most of the houses in town. The lower area has a simple mud floor that has been compacted over time into an almost tile-like hardness. There is storage and a place for cooking. A large trough for hay is also here, but there are no animals in the house. Some small slit windows let the smoke from the cooking escape. In the very back are stairs leading up through an opening to the second floor. The man motions for Barry to come up the stairs. As they enter the second floor, Barry sees a woman who looks like the man's wife and two daughters. There is also an older man and older woman that Barry assumes are the parents of either the 'barrel man' or the wife. There is a small wooden table with chairs in the middle of the room. Towards the back are three doorways which are partially concealed with linen drapes. A small loom sits against one wall with a piece of fabric in progress interlaced and hanging to one side. There are small windows that are also concealed by curtains which are backlit from the setting sun. The smallest daughter is lighting oil lamps.

The man sits down and motions to Barry to sit next to him. The oldest daughter comes with a bowl and towel to wash the man's feet. She then comes to wash Barry's feet. Barry stares at her as she cannot help but stare back at him. She fumbles with the cloths and almost spills the water as she finishes but is still staring. Barry begins to feel uncomfortable as he notices that everyone begins to stare at him. Soon, everyone is sitting at the table. The older woman comes and sits down with little effort, but the older man has to be helped to the table. Once everybody is settled, the man begins to pray. Barry can pick out words here and there from the man's liturgy. It's in Hebrew, but again, it is slightly different from the scholarly Hebrew Barry learned in school. As quickly as it begins, it is over and everyone is beginning to pass food around.

The man takes a bowl that contains some kind of stew. He looks at Barry and says another word slowly holding up the stew. Barry repeats the word back to him. It causes giggles from the two girls who are quickly chastised by the father. Barry puts some of the stew onto his plate and hands the bowl to the older daughter sitting next to him. For reasons unknown to Barry, he says the word to the girl as he is passing the bowl. The girls now choke on their laughter as they glance to the father. But even the 'barrel man' begins to laugh at this and the two girls bust out with giggles once more. This time, as quietly as possible. "I feel like such an idiot," Barry thinks. "But I don't care. This food smells too good and I'm too hungry." Barry tries to restrain himself and not eat too quickly as to not look like a pig. But this is the first real meal he has eaten in a very long time and the stew was surprising tasty. Barry ends up eating all that is left, which also solicits stifled giggles from the girls.

Soon the meal is over and the 'barrel man' says something to the two daughters. Barry cannot help but notice that they have a stare of almost disbelief as their eyes open wider and they're frozen in place. After a short, awkward silence, the father says something again in a stronger voice. This snaps the girls out of their trance and they quickly retreat down the stairs as they are watched by the father. He turns back and pats Barry on the shoulder with what sounds like an apology, as if Barry would know if it was or not. In about ten minutes, the girls return and go racing past Barry, disappearing behind the drapes. The man motions to Barry as he gets up out of the chair. "Come," he says. That's one of the few words Barry knows without hesitation now. Barry follows the man back down the stairs to the lower floor and over to the animal trough. It is filled with hay covered with a blanket as the daughters have prepared it. The man tells Barry another word as he pats the blanket. He puts his hands together up next to his head and makes that 'sleep' motion that you make to kids.

"This is where I'm to sleep?" Barry ponders. The light bulb finally switches on. "I get it now. This wasn't a 'move-a-barrel-for-a-coin' job. This man wants help and he figures that I'm the only unemployed person in town. He's giving me a job. That rabbi was here to bless the whole arrangement. I get it now." Barry points to the blanket and then to himself. The man nods his head and smiles a little smirk of a smile. "It is true. I'm not a beggar anymore. I can work for a living now... and this guy will teach me what I need to know. What a fantastic day this has turned out to be!" An uncontainable smile erupts onto Barry's face. The man turns to go back up the stairs. In a flood of emotion, Barry grabs the man in a giant bear-hug. The man is startled, but then smirks again with a tiny smile. As Barry release him, he nods at Barry and pats him on the shoulder. As he turns to leave he points to the trough as if to say, "Get some sleep." After the man returns up the stairs, Barry is still standing there unable to believe that this has happened. "My whole life has changed once more. God has humbled me and now given me a second chance at a meaningful life."

He moves to the bed and pushes down on the blanket. The hay feels soft. He loosens and removes his cloth girdle, slips off his sandals and lies down. It is soft. He has slept on the cold hard ground for so long; he's forgotten how soft a bed can feel. This is so much better. Then Barry remembers his blankets and box. Even though they are old, ratty blankets, Barry quietly slips out the doorway and makes his way back to his spot by the synagogue. There are his blankets and box, right where he left them. On the blanket and in the dirt next to the blanket are three coins. Barry wonders if the people who dropped them even noticed that he was gone. He gathers up his belongings and makes his way back to the 'barrel man's house'. On the way back, he asks himself, "So, why did I have to come back for these? I dreamed of the day I could leave these behind, and now I go get them. Maybe it's because – no matter who you are – you still have to have your 'stuff'."

Barry puts the box under the trough. He rolls up the smaller blanket to use like a pillow and uses the larger blanket to cover his feet and legs. The bed feels so good that it doesn't take Barry long to drift off to sleep, happy with his new life.

ANOTHER DAY IN TIMNAH

Barry wakes up and stretches his arms and legs out as he's awaken by the movement of thumping feet on the upper floor. He quickly gets up and puts on his girdle and his sandals. He grabs a broom and begins to sweep out the lower floor. The women will be down soon to start breakfast. He sweeps the dust to the doorway and looks out. The sun is just peering over the horizon and in the distance a cock is crowing. "Another beautiful day, it looks like," Barry thinks to himself. It is reaching summer again and the high temperatures for the days are rising. He returns to his sweeping.

About a year and a half slips by for Barry since Alon brought him here. Alon is the blacksmith, but Barry calls him 'Ed' inside his head because he reminds Barry of an Ed from back home. Since Barry's brain is still attached to the twenty-first century, he gives everyone in the family names he can relate to in his mind. First, there is Ed. He's almost six foot tall and is in his early to mid-thirties, only about seven to ten years older than Barry. He is a hard worker and a very kind man with a big heart. The patience that he shows in teaching Barry is truly remarkable in Barry's estimation. Then there is Migda, who Barry calls 'Mary'. She's Ed's wife and not a bad cook. She is around thirty as well and stands about the same height as Barry, around five foot nine. She is a slender woman with a pretty face and straight, jet black hair. There are the two daughters, Shira and Bracha, who Barry has named 'Susan' and 'Betty' respectively. Susan is in her mid-teens and a spitting image of her mother, a real heart-breaker. She has the same straight black hair and the biggest, brown, puppy-dog eyes. Betty, on the other hand, favors Ed with her lighter, curly hair. She's about ten years old and thinks that most of the things that Barry does are funny. After some time, Barry figures out that the older woman, Ditza, is Mary's mother. She is pretty spry for her age and is always directing the work, to Mary's exasperation. Barry just thinks of her as 'Grams'. The older man is Ezra, Ed's father. He dies during the winter. Barry can tell they still miss him from time to time. They all live in a town called Timnah. Barry can recall the name from his studies but is unsure exactly where he is in relation to Jerusalem.

Barry sports a new tunic; at least it was new about three months ago. Mary makes it for him and Ed burns the old one. Barry thinks it's because there is too much beggar smell in it. On Barry's one year anniversary with Ed, he was given a leather girdle with pockets to put around his waist and some new sandals. Susan trims his beard on occasion and also cuts his hair from time to time.

It's a new routine from what Barry had as a beggar. He cleans the lower floor and then eats breakfast with the family. Ed then takes him around and gives him things to do. Barry has learned how to patch pots, sharpen tools, load the furnace, and assemble and disassemble plows. But most of what Barry does is clean up Ed's messes. That's every day except the Sabbath. On that evening, the work stops and Barry enters the doorway to find his dinner waiting for him on the bed. The rest of the family goes upstairs and Barry doesn't see them again until morning. He eats his dinner and leaves the dishes next to the hearth. Most of the time, he spends his day off just walking through the town and watching people. Now that Ed has help, the work gets finished faster. So, on most days, Barry climbs the narrow stairs on the outside of the house to the flat roof on top that is covered with a cloth canopy and watches the sunset. Susan takes to watching it with him when she can. At first, they sit on opposite sides of the bench and Susan seems somewhat tense. Barry has a vocabulary for everyday chores and objects. He still struggles to make complete thoughts. In Barry's mind, he sounds like the old cowboy western movie Indian. "How... you go... me stay... sweep'em floor..." But, Barry's able to get by and he's improving over time. Ed teaches him how and where to do business in town and familiarizes Barry with the local monetary system. A lot of the farmers still use wooden plows with metal fittings, but Ed builds a metal one every now and then. He makes a lot of bronze pots and vessels of various shapes and sizes. Most of the iron he works is for tools and fittings.

On this day, Barry climbs the stairs and looks out to the horizon. "Another day gone. Such a long way from the fame and fortune I came here for. It's a certainty that I'll never strike it rich here. I guess I shouldn't complain. At least I'm alive. I eat well enough and I have a dry place to sleep when it rains. Never thought that would be as important to me as it is. But then, I should already be dead... twice." Then Barry adds with a sigh, "I just wish I knew what I was doing here?"

Susan and Betty climb to the roof to join Barry. Susan hands Barry some wine in a clay cup and today sits down next to him on the bench. This garners a giggle from Betty, who sits down on the roof next to the bench. Susan lays her head on Barry's shoulder. "I wish I could make better small talk," Barry thinks. But instead, they all sit silent in the moment and enjoy the sunset until Mary calls them to dinner.

It is winter and the rains have come. Most of the work stops and it becomes a very boring existence for Barry. One day Barry is standing in the doorway looking out into the gently falling rain. "I came here looking for Jesus. I wonder if he's even out there. God? If you would have any mercy on me, answer my one prayer. If Jesus is out there, I want to see him. I want to know that I didn't come all this way for nothing. That I didn't throw my life away to be a poor blacksmith's assistant. Even if I can't take the proof back to my time, just let me see him." As Barry stand there lost in thought, he is suddenly shoved out into the rain. He turns to run back into the doorway and sees a squealing Betty running back up the stairs.

The next day, Barry is working outside and Betty comes and tugs on Barry's sleeve. "Come," Betty says as she continues to tug. "Yes," Barry says and follows Betty upstairs. It is almost lunch and the sky is grey and trying to decide if it will rain yet again. Everyone is gathered around the table. Barry sits down along with Betty. Ed starts to say something about Susan. Barry can pick out enough to suspect that Susan is sixteen years old today. She looks so grown up and has a huge smile on her face. Mary brings out some kind of food Barry had never seen. The plate has several small biscuit-looking cakes on it. Mary hands one to Barry and he becomes aware that everyone is watching for him to take the first bite. It smells good and as Barry bites into it. It is sweet. An uncommon occurrence in the dietary patterns he had seen so far. "Ummm... Good!" Barry says and the girls giggle as they reach for one.

There is more conversation and then Ed says something and Barry sees the smile disappear from Susan's face. There is an uneasy silence as Barry can see tears welling up in Susan's eyes and she suddenly bolts from the table and back to her room. Mary swats at Ed and it breaks out into what sounds to Barry like a small argument which ends when Mary heads off to Susan's room too. "What wrong?" Barry asks.

Ed, looking like he wants to back what he said if he could, shakes his head and sighs, "Too old... No husband." Ed grabs at one of the cakes and pops it into his mouth half-heartedly. He puts his elbow on the table, rests his head in his hand and stares off to nothing in particular.

Barry gets up and slowly walks back downstairs. He goes outside and takes the stairs to the roof as it appears the rain will hold off one more day. "I had never thought about it. But he's right. Sixteen is old in this culture to not be married. And she doesn't have a lot of prospects." Barry walks through the town all the time and sees lots of girls and not that many boys the same age as Susan. "Most of the boys in town are Betty's age," Barry continues to muse. "Betty will have a much easier time when that day comes. But Susan doesn't stand much of a chance to snag a boy here. And from what I've seen, none of these boys are the pick of the litter either. What a tough break... to be an old maid at sixteen... poor kid." Soon, Susan appears with slightly swollen, red eyes. She sits down next to Barry and Barry puts his arm around her.

"Sorry," is all Barry knows to say.

"Be not sorry," Susan says as she shakes her head.

"I wish I could comfort her," Barry thinks. "But I have no words for that." But just to sit and share the moment seems to be comfort enough for now.

JUST A SLAVE

It is spring; another Hanukkah come and gone. For Barry, another Christmas come and gone. He laughs whenever he thinks about the paradox. Should he miss celebrating a birthday for a Messiah that might not have even been born yet? There was no way to know, but still he prays that it might come to pass that he would meet Jesus. It is a pleasant day and Barry is patching yet another small hole in a bronze pot. He hears a noise in the distance, but takes no notice of it at first. It is a faint rumble like the sound of thunder at the edge of the horizon. But as it starts to grow louder, it clamors for Barry's attention until it can no longer be ignored. Barry stops his work and looks to the sound trying to figure out what it is. "What is that?" Barry ponders. "I've never heard a noise like that since I've been here. It can't be a storm; there isn't a cloud in the sky. It's getting louder and now I think I can hear a distinct pounding."

Ed comes scurrying through the gate to the courtyard. He has a frightened look on his face that Barry has also never seen before. As Barry starts to say something about the sound, Ed runs past him and grabs him by the sleeve. He pulls on Barry so hard, that Barry stumbles backwards and almost falls. It does not seem to deter Ed, as he yanks on Barry and says, "Come." Once inside, he yells something to Mary and they begin shutting the shutters to the windows upstairs. Mary then shoos the girls into their room and disappears with Grams into the other doorway.

Ed cracks open one of the shutters and peeks out. Barry positions his head towards the bottom of the window so he can also see out. Suddenly, the source of the commotion becomes clear. Barry sees a column of Roman soldiers marching on the road. "Wow!" Barry almost blurts out. "Look at that! An actual Roman legion... how cool is that?" Barry looks on like a small boy at the circus. He marvels as the column advances down the road, their spears bobbing up and down with each step. Their shields radiating the sun's light and flashing as they rock back and forth. The noise of their synchronized moment pounding the air into an almost deafening cacophony of sounds. "Truly amazing. To actually be able to see the things you've only read about," Barry thinks. "To be marching to battle as a ragged militia and to hear this pounding and see the light beaming off them would have struck a certain amount of fear in to anyone, I guess."

He glances up to Ed and Ed lowers his face to see Barry. When Barry sees the horrified look still on Ed's face, Barry's sheepish grin feels out of place and it fades quickly from his face. "I have forgotten where I am," Barry thinks. As he turns to sit on the floor with his back to the wall, the situation becomes all too clear. "They are the enemy. They are the force occupying this land. I've never known what it's like to live under another government's rule. To be a subject of a foreign power." Barry looks back at Ed again as Ed stares out the crack. "Working here day to day, it is so easy to forget that I am living under occupation. You don't think about it… or at least, I didn't think about it. But it's all too real to them. It's the only thing they've ever known. I wonder if something happened at this town in the past. Had the Romans torn up the place and killed people? Or was it normal to cower this way every time the enemy marches through?" Barry can faintly hear the hooves of horses passing outside as well.

"I'm a conquered subject – a slave - just like them now. Except… I'm not like them. I'm a slave to this family as well," Barry's mind races. "Why haven't I realized this before? I'm a slave… or least a servant. I like that word better. But it's the same thing. I belong to Ed now, there's no other possibility. He doesn't pay me… I work for room and board. I can't be just an indentured servant, because Ed would have to free me once I paid my debt. But I don't have a debt. Or if my room and board is a debt, I'll never be able to repay it. I have to eat and with every meal, I'm indebted again."

The noise is dying off. Ed tugs at Barry and says, "Come… quiet." Barry gets up and follows Ed downstairs. Carefully, Ed makes his way out onto the road, followed closely by Barry. A couple of the neighbors also come out onto the road. Then as a group, everyone begins to make their way up the road following the Romans and being careful not to run up the back of the column. The group stops at the town's center and are joined by more men. After the sounds of the Romans fade into the afternoon air, there is a meeting of men that have come to the center of town. After some discussion, it appears the threat is over and there is a collective sigh from the group assembled. Ed, looking much more at ease now, tugs at Barry and says, "Come… go home," as they make their way home. That evening, Barry sits next to Susan but his thoughts are far from the sunset. He is still fixated on his epiphany.

"I can't believe I'm a slave. But on the other hand, what's wrong with being a slave? I have as much of a family as I could ask for. They feed me and take care of me... I have work... Does it matter if I'm not getting paid? Even if I could leave, where would I go?" Barry is snapped out of his trance by Susan who gets up and begins to wave her hand in front of Barry's face. Barry apologizes and says goodnight to Susan as she and Betty go back down the stairs. That night, as Barry lies in his bed, staring at the ceiling, he decides, "Slave or not, I couldn't do any better than I am now. So, if I must be a slave, then I will be happy and continue on."

Barry has little time to get used to being a slave to Ed. As it turns out, this is the Jubilee Year. One year in seven when some slaves are given their freedom. Late in the summer, the rabbi comes by as Ed and Barry work in the courtyard. Ed greets the rabbi and begins to talk to him while, all the time, pointing to Barry. The rabbi and Ed call to Barry and the three of them go into the house. The rabbi starts to examine Barry with a slow eye, like a jeweler looking for flaws in a precious stone. He then asks Barry to lift up his tunic. "What? What is this guy up to?" ponders Barry. Barry complies and lifts up his tunic slightly as he looks around expecting one of the girls to pop in. "Higher," the rabbi says. Barry keeps raising it up until the bottom is at his waist." The rabbi then grabs for Barry's loincloth and jerks it down. They appear to be talking about Barry's private parts and then the examination is over. As they continue to discuss, Barry comes to the realization that they are checking to see if he has been circumcised. They want to know if Barry is 'Jewish'. The rabbi nods his head, turns and says some words towards

Barry while raising his hands. He then departs as quickly as he came.

As Barry stands stunned watching this entire spectacle take place and the rabbi walking away, he says a small prayer of thanks to his parents, "Thanks mom and dad. I would hate to have to undergo that now…" Ed slaps him on the shoulder and says, "You… man… today." At first Barry is unsure exactly what that means, but he soon figures out that he is freed from his servant hood. "You… name… Oded," Ed declares.

"Oded? Why?" Barry asked.

"New life… new name."

That makes sense to Barry. It is not uncommon to change names because of a life changing event. Much like Saul became Paul upon his conversion or how Simon became known better as Peter. Barry also believes that Ed never got used to 'Barry' as a name.

Ed begins to pay him now, but then takes back most of it. Barry figures that is payment for room and board now. Barry is convinced that it is Ed's way of teaching him the economics of the day. Barry is now invited upstairs on the Sabbath. Even though he doesn't understand everything, Barry is grateful to be an even greater part of the family. Now, if he wanted to, he could leave and search for Jesus, if he's out there. But, it is a thought that Barry never takes seriously. He is still too dependent on Ed and this family to get by. He also finds the thought of leaving painful. There is something he can't explain that keeps him here. But he continues to pray for the day when he might catch even a glimpse of Jesus.

A DESPERATE FLIGHT

It is warmer than average as winter creeps closer. Susan is sick. It started about two weeks prior. Barry notices that Susan is not acting right, she is very tired and misses sitting with Barry three evenings in a row. Then she starts to cough. Today, she is in bed with a fever. Everyone is trying their best to carry on, but Ed is often distracted as he struggles to complete even simple tasks. He goes into the house often to check on her. Barry, too, finds it difficult to concentrate on his work. Ed comes out and tells Barry, "Shira… see you… go in."

Barry enters the darkened room and the air hangs heavy and still. The shutters are closed and covered and a single oil lamp struggles to fight back the darkness. Mary is rinsing out a cloth in a water basin and places it on Susan's head. Barry waits for Mary and then moves to sit on the edge of the bed. Barry puts his hand on Susan's face and she strains to open her eyes. She smiles a weak little smile when she sees Barry and places her hand on his. "Oded," Susan says in a weak voice. She is taken by the fever and is very warm to the touch. The color is drained out of her.

The adoring little face with the big puppy dog eyes is now ashen and the dim light is not enough to hide the look of despair and fear in Susan's face. She is dying and she knows it.

Barry does his best to smile and say, "Everything... be good... soon." But, it doesn't seem to bring her comfort as she coughs again.

"Miss...sunsets," Susan struggles to get out as she continues to try and hold onto Barry's hand on her face.

"Sunset.... miss... you," Barry says softly.

Susan manages a smile, but it is short lived. She starts to cough and hack again. With every attack, her body looks even frailer and life seems to be slipping away. She drifts in and out of sleep as Barry thinks, "I'm no doctor, but this look like nothing more than influenza. This is something so treatable in my day and now, here I sit, helpless... watching her die. If I could just run down to the corner drugstore and get her some antibiotics, she would probably live through this." Susan moans and writhes before dropping back into a sleep. Mary takes the cloth and dunks it back into the water and wrings it out. She places it across Susan's head again. Barry takes hold of Susan's hand and holds it to him. "Dear God," he prays silently, "why must you take her life? This is my only family now. I give you this solemn vow. I will do anything you ask if you will just save her. If there is any justice left and this whole fiasco is to come to anything, then let her live." Susan slips back into a deep sleep and Mary shoos Barry from the room.

The next day, Ed's neighbor Shlomo comes through the gate shouting to Ed. Ed greets him and they begin to talk as Barry looks on. "Wonder what's on ol' Mo's mind?" Barry muses. "Whatever it is, Mo is sure wound up about it." Soon, the men part and Shlomo leaves. Ed comes walking past Barry with the first hint of a smile since Susan became ill. "Tonight... fix Susan." Ed says as he heads into the house. "Fix Susan?" Barry ponders. "Maybe ol' Mo has invented penicillin." Then Barry's thoughts return to Susan as she grows weaker day by day. "I don't know what he's got in mind, but it better be good."

That night, Shlomo brings his donkey and wagon to the gate. It is the same small wagon that Barry helped Ed unload all those months ago. Ed hands Barry some tools and grabs some wood and says, "Come!" They go to the wagon and begin to fashion a very crude frame that is then covered with cloth to make a canopy cover for the wagon. They throw together a trough like shape and load it with hay. Ed goes inside as Barry finishes tying everything down. Ed emerges from the house carrying Susan and lays her in the wagon. He is followed by Mary and Betty as they bring baskets of food and jars of wine. Mary hands Barry a large bowl containing some water and a rag. Barry climbs into the back of the wagon and begins to care for Susan. Ed hugs his wife and daughter and climbs up into the wagon and grabs the reigns. Suddenly, they are off racing into the darkness.

"Where go?" asks Barry.

"Find rabbi... fix Shira..." replies Ed.

"Rabbi? Here?"

"No," Ed says. And then he says something that catches Barry by surprise.

"Wait... That Hebrew word Ed just used could be translated as 'Messiah'. Can we be looking for Jesus?" Barry's mind races. "That has to be it. Nothing else makes sense. We're looking for a rabbi that can heal the sick. That has to be Jesus. Maybe God decided to answer all my prayers after all." Barry's ecstasy is quickly snuffed as Susan begins to moan with the jostling of the cart. "Hang in there, Susan," Barry whispers. "You've got to make it."

The wagon rolls on into the night as the oil lamp on the front splits open the curtain of darkness which closes back behind them. As the lights of Timnah fade into the blackness, there is an eeriness that surrounds the wagon. There is no moon this night and Ed urges on the donkey as fast as he can see the road ahead. Time seems to stand still, but Barry knows that Susan doesn't have much left. Her moans are now comforting as they provide evidence she is still fighting.

As dawn comes, the oil is out and the last several hours have gone at what feels like a snail's pace because Ed can barely see anything ahead of the donkey. The wagon comes to a stop next to a watering pond. Ed says, "Get water." He and Barry both get down from the wagon and head to the water's edge. Barry fills up the water jug and Ed fills a wide, shallow bucket and hauls it over to the donkey. The donkey drinks the water stopping only to chew on the nearby vegetation. Barry climbs into the wagon and dips the rag into some of the cold water and places in on Susan's head. The coldness elicits a large moan and she is able to crack open her eyes. Barry put his hand under her head and lifts her up to get her to take a small drink. She is able to take a small sip before dropping back into unconsciousness. Ed climbs back into the wagon and uncovers the food. He pours some wine into a glass and, after drinking some, passes it to Barry. Ed tears off some bread and gives it to Barry. As Barry bites into the bread, he realizes how hungry he is. The whole trip has been spent hanging on Susan's every breath and his nerves are frayed. Barry cannot fall asleep for he is afraid he will lose her if he sleeps. The fruit and bread renew his energy. Soon, they are on their way again. Ed is pushing the donkey now as he knows Susan is close to death. Before long, there is a town that appears on the horizon along with a rising sun. With even more urgency, Ed urges the donkey to faster speed.

As they arrive, this is a much bigger town than Timnah. The streets are narrow and crowded. The air here is stale and motionless and there is a pungent aroma that grows the deeper into the city one goes. Ed finds a place to pull the wagon to a halt. He yells to several bystanders that hurry to the wagon. They pick up Susan and move her off the wagon. As they cradle her in their arms like a stretcher, they begin to move quickly up the street. Barry jumps from the wagon and begins to follow, but Ed stops him and says, "Wait… water food… donkey." Barry nods and Ed runs up the street after his daughter as they duck around a corner and disappear from sight. Barry is exhausted and his mind is numb. It's been a little more than twenty-four hours since he slept. He loosens the bridle on the donkey. He goes to a nearby well and fills the donkey's bucket. He puts down some feed on the ground and then bends over and begins to rub on the donkey's head as it eats. "You did it," Barry whispers to the donkey, his ears alert as he eats and drinks. "You got us here. Now if Jesus is really here, maybe we're in time. We can only…" Barry is cut off and stands up stiff as two women walk by and begin to stare at him. Once the women have passed, Barry relaxes again. "Yep," he continues, "we can only wait and see." He pats the donkey's head and rubs on its neck. "I'm going to name you Ruffy… after the dog I had when I was a boy. I could always count on him to be there too. You don't mind that name, do you? No?… Ok." Barry leaves the donkey eating and grabs a small piece of fruit from the front of the wagon and pours a small amount of wine. He walks around to the back of the wagon. He sits in the back leaning on one of the makeshift posts so that he can see up the street where they took Susan and eats his meager breakfast. After he has finished, his eyes get heavy, his head periodically jolts as he pops awake. As some point, Barry loses his battle and falls asleep.

"Oded!" Barry hears in a far off tone.

"That's me, I think… yeah, that is me," Barry begins to think as he's still half asleep. "Who's calling me? It sounds like… Susan." Barry eyes pop open as he realizes it is Susan's voice he hears. He tries to sit up but his muscles protest as he's been sitting in this position too long and his body is stiff.

"Oded!" the voice comes again.

Barry tries to climb off the wagon, stumbles and almost falls. As he regains focus, it is close to noon and the sun is high in the sky. He's been asleep for about four to five hours. He looks up the street and Susan is running back to the wagon followed in the distance by Ed. He can't believe his eyes. It's as if she had never been ill. He begins to run towards her as she draws near. Barry is so happy; he scoops her up in his arms and starts to twirl her around in a circle. Susan is surprised and lets out a small squeak of a noise followed by a small laugh as she places her hands on Barry's face. He brings her to rest on her feet once more as Ed comes walking up with a large smile that only a father could have in this situation. Ed and Barry briefly hug in joy before Ed yawns a big yawn and starts to stretch. He's been up far longer than Barry and is now feeling it. "I can't believe it," Barry thinks to himself. "I'm so happy Susan is well. I guess I have God to thank… and Jesus…" It is at that very moment that Barry begins to shake. It is one of those 'forest-for-the-trees' type of moments. Barry begins to panic, "Wait! Jesus! He's here? He must be here! That's the only explanation! I have to see him! I can't have missed him… Oh, please God, don't let me have missed him." Barry runs over and yanks on Ed's arm as he begins to climb up into the wagon.

"What, Oded?" asks a bewildered Ed.

"Where!?!" Barry shouts out in an uncontrollable excitement.

"Where?" quizzes Ed.

Barry was having trouble finding the words as he stammers and his thought process is in 'lockdown'. "Why can't you understand English for ten seconds!" Barry screams in his head. "Where... Shira... fix? Where?"

Ed tries to point the way, but Barry starts to drag him up the street from where Ed and Susan had come. Finally Ed figures out he will have to show Barry and they both scurry off.

They come to a small plaza between buildings. There is a man standing and speaking. Ed points to this man and then turns to go back saying, "Wagon... sleep." Barry stands motionless watching this man as he addresses the crowd of people that have squeezed into this plaza. "Is that him?" Barry ponders. "Can that be Jesus? Now I know why Judas had to kiss him to identify him to the authorities. He looks exactly like everyone sitting down listening to him. This can't be Jesus... I didn't expect the neatly trimmed goatee and straight blonde hair... but this man is so... ordinary." Barry moves a little closer but not into the plaza. "But this is the man who healed Susan. He's the one Ed pointed out. It's got to be him. Now that I'm here, I feel myself filled with doubt. How is he going to help me anyway? Can he send me back home?"

At that moment, the man's eyes fall on Barry. He stops talking for a moment as he stares intently and directly at Barry and a small smirk seems to come across his face. After what seems like a very long break to Barry but is really only a short pause, the man resumes speaking. Barry gasps for breath. "He saw me... He knows who I am," Barry's mind begins to overflow with thoughts. "He knows I'm here. He knows who I am and where I come from... I know he knows... That look he had, it was like he was saying to me, 'So, you finally found me, did you?' It has to be Jesus. He can help me... he has to... he's the only one who can. I have to speak to him."

The man finishes speaking and, as he stands there, the crowds begin to get up and disperse. The man takes another look at Barry and then begins to walk away. Barry can no longer control himself and his desperation takes over. "Jesus!" Barry yells at the top of his voice as he begins to run towards the man. The man stops and turns around. "Jesus! You have to help me, please!" Barry continues to scream as he runs. Almost everyone in the crowd is frozen as they watch this madman rushing towards the man who has been speaking and yelling in a non-discernable tongue. A few try to stop Barry from reaching him, but Barry goes through them like an NFL running back on a Sunday afternoon. As he gets to the man who is staring at him, Barry stops and stares into his eyes. He and the man are now face to face as the crowd looks on and a peaceful calm comes over Barry. He drops to his knees and looks up at the man who continues to stare back.

"I know you are Jesus," Barry says in tearful tone. "I know that you know what I'm saying. You're the only one who does. You're the only one who can help me. Please, take pity on your servant and show me mercy. I will do whatever it is you ask. I swear. I swear it, whatever you ask. But you must help me. I need to be home... Please? I need to be home." The tears are now streaming down Barry's face. The man smiles a small smile and, without a word, places his hands on either side of Barry's head. Barry continues to plead, "You must help me, I need to be home," as the man's glare gets more intense.

Suddenly, Barry's voice stops. He can feel something inside his head. At first, it is uncomfortable. But soon it starts to tingle and burn. Barry's face winces a couple of times and he can feel the stabbing pain getting stronger. Barry places his hands on the man's hands as the pain increases and now feels like a searing blade has been thrust into his head. Barry starts to cry out as the pain continues to increase. Then, as suddenly as it appeared, the pain subsides and Barry is left with a head that is tingling to the touch. He stares into the man's eyes and asks, "What?... What did you do to me?"

"Only what you have asked in faith," he replies.

The man removes his hands and Barry's body slumps down as his energy is depleted and his head still tingles. The man turns and begins to leave. Barry watches him walk away and begins to feel his head with his hands. "What did he do to me?" ponders Barry. "My head doesn't feel any different... there's no blood... I'm still here, I'm not home. If he didn't do anything to me, why is my head tingling? I don't understand." Barry looks up and the man is now gone. "Maybe it was all a dream."

"Hey? Are you alright now?" a nearby observer asks.

"What do you mean? What happened to me?" Barry asks, still bewildered.

"Look!" shouts another, "The master has driven out this man's demons."

"Demons?" quips Barry rubbing his head, "I didn't have..." Then Barry's head pops up and his eyes get really big. He stands up and grabs the bystander that had spoken to him. "What did you say?" The bystander becomes frightened and doesn't say anything. "Say something to me... anything," Barry demands.

"Don't hurt me. I was not the one who said you have demons," replies the man sheepishly.

Barry suddenly hugs the man and said, "I can understand you!" A giddy, almost maniacal, laughter swells up in Barry as he begins to jump around and dance. "I've been saved! Praise God! It's a miracle. Do you hear me? A miracle!" He continues jumping and dancing down the street. He stops another person and demands, "Say something to me!"

"What do you want me to say to you?" the stranger asks.

"Amazing! Jesus healed me. He's the Messiah and he took away the weight of the world!" Barry yells and continues to run and jump and dance. Then he stops in front of a store front. "I can read the sign!" he yells and points and again begins to jump and dance. He tells everyone he can find what has happened. Most seem content to let him rave and then dismiss him as crazy. He goes until his strength gives out and then he sits in the road and rests. Once his strength returns, he begins the cycle all over again.

Barry stops on a street and sits down. Once again he feels his head with his hands. "How did he do it? Jesus not only reprogrammed my brain but my knowledge as well. I not only can speak and read, I somehow understand the customs and I know the traditions. Even without having lived through them. It's not possible, and yet he did it. How could I document such a miracle? Even if the whole project had been successful, how do I describe what he did to me?" He dances for a couple of hours and then remembers his companions at the wagon. Barry returns to them hoping they had not left for home yet.

When Barry arrives back at the place where they had stopped, the wagon is still there, now in the shade of late afternoon. Alon and Shira are sleeping in the back, unnoticed by those rushing to finish their business before dark. Barry quietly walks up to the wagon and looks at Shira. Her angelic face is once again as it should be. Barry just stands for a while looking at her sleep. "Shira," whispers Barry as he nudges her gently.

"Oded," she says as she wakes up and rubs her eyes, "where...go? What...you...do?" Barry has to laugh now. He can see why Bracha is always laughing at him as he now knows how primitive he sounded. Her beautiful smile turns to a perplexed frown as Barry chuckles uncontrollably.

"Oh, Shira," Barry says sweetly, "how I have longed to be able to talk with you."

"Oded!" Shira squeaks as her eyes grow wide and her mouth hangs open. Slowly her familiar smile crawls back onto her face. "Papa! Papa wake up!" she says excitedly as she shakes Alon awake.

"What is it, my daughter? Why did you wake me?" Alon gruffs as he rubs his head and tries to regain his bearings.

"It's Oded!" Shira says pointing to Barry.

"I can see that, Shira. What does he want?"

"I want to go home. We should leave now before it gets dark." Barry says calmly.

"What? How...?" Alon can barely squeeze out before a large smile also finds its way onto his face. "How can you talk now?"

"It was Jesus," exclaims Barry. "Just as he healed Shira, he made my mind whole again."

"What a day it has been." Alon cries out. "You are right, Oded. We should head home."

"Won't mama and Bracha be surprised," Shira beams as Alon and Barry ready the wagon again.

Alon takes his place and turns the donkey back on the road. Barry and Shira sit in the back and talk about all that has happened. She wants to know Barry's history and about his childhood. Barry knows he can't tell her. She would not understand and even the language lacks words to describe half of Barry's world. Barry tells them that he can't remember much of his 'previous life' before being found and brought to Timnah. They seem to accept that excuse quite readily and don't question it as they exit the town, Shira tells Barry all about her childhood with comments from Alon.

THE HAUNTING PULL

Barry stops his work as his stares out to nothing in particular and his thoughts wander. "It was him. It was Jesus... I never got a chance to thank him for what he did. Although he probably knows... being Jesus and all... I never got a chance to ask any of the questions I have always wanted to ask. So, will I ever get to see him again? I wonder where he's at in his ministry... is the time close? It has to be close. There were only a few years. There are so many things in my mind now..." Barry snaps out of his daydream when Alon puts his hand on Barry's shoulder. "Oh, sorry," Barry says apologetically. "I was just lost in thought."

"Quite often, I've noticed. You're thinking about this Jesus? This prophet?" Alon suggests.

"He's more than a prophet. He's the Messiah. I have so many questions and I can't stop thinking about it. When I stared into his eyes..." Barry says as his concentration wanes away.

"Maybe it's time for you to leave me then."

"Oh, no. I owe everything to you, Alon. You are the only family I have now. It would be hard for me to leave here as well."

"You know, Oded, if you have been called to follow God, you cannot refuse. Would you make yourself Jonah?"

Barry knows that Alon is right. He will never find peace here now. "You are right, Alon. I must leave. I'm sorry." But Barry finds the thought of leaving to be disturbing too.

"What is there to be sorry about? To be called by God is an honor. One that no good man would pass up. But, before you leave, I must ask something of you."

"Anything. I would do anything for you."

"Sit down, Oded," Alon says. As Barry sits on a stool in the courtyard, Alon takes a quick look around to make sure they are alone. "Do you love Shira?"

"Uhhh…" is all Barry can manage. "Love?" he thinks to himself, "'Do I love her?' he asked… She's a child, only sixteen… well, almost seventeen now. On the other hand, she's more mature than some women I've known at twenty-something. If I'm honest with myself, she is the one I would miss the most. She's the reason I find it hard to leave here. Do I love her?" Barry looks back to Alon and says, "Yes. I think I do love her."

"She loves you also. I overhear her and her mother talking."

"Really?" Barry muses.

"I would like you to take her as your wife…" Alon proposes. Alon keeps talking after that, but Barry hears none of it.

"Wife!" Barry thinks as his mind races again. "Me marry Shira? No, that's just too creepy. I'm almost twenty-eight. She's seventeen. But then, it was not unusual to select an older man that could provide for the woman. She's very unlikely to find a husband here with the lack of prospects.

And Alon wants to make sure he has an heir as well, I'm guessing. And she loves me. But I'm going... I'm leaving... I'm hitting the road. Do I want to drag a young girl around with me? But, on the other hand, even the apostles had wives. But we're from two different worlds. And yet, in the end, I can't imagine this one without her. From the day we got back from making her well, I've thought about her as much as I've thought about Jesus. She's my best tie to this world."

"You're a good man, I know you'll take care of her," Alon says finishing up his little speech. Barry looks at him as if he has heard everything Alon has said. The thought of leaving Shira was now unthinkable to Barry.

"I have saved some, but I do not have enough money for a bride price."

"You helped me save her life, Oded. I could not be paid any more than that."

Barry stands and says, "I will take Shira to be my wife."

Alon hugs Barry and turns to go into the house. "I will tell Migda the news," he says and then disappears through the doorway. Barry sinks back down onto the stool.

"What have I done?" Barry ponders. It's no time at all until Shira comes running from the house. Barry has never seen her beam so brightly. He stands with arms open, but is almost knocked back over the stool from the force of Shira's leap into his arms. They embrace as he holds her tightly to himself. A new found peace sweeps over Barry as he holds her in his arms. "Yep, I guess I have no choice to admit it," Barry thinks, "I do love her."

Barry and Shira are now betrothed. There is a great celebration at Alon's house. Soon, Barry and Shira stand beneath the wedding tent and they drink wine from the cup that seals them together as bride and groom with half the town gathered around. Since Barry has no father in

Timnah, Shlomo volunteers to be Barry's surrogate father and opens his home to include their wedding chamber. After the wedding, the bride goes back to her father's house to gather her things and to be prepared to be a wife. The groom goes back to his father's house to prepare a place to stay. Usually, this is a permanent arrangement and they will live in the father's house until the son inherits it. Because of this, the waiting period can be up to twelve months as the young girl is trained and permanent living quarters are built. But, as both Barry and Shira are leaving after the wedding and Shira is of an age that she has already been training for years, the rabbi gives permission for the time to be greatly abbreviated.

Soon, Barry has prepared a room in Shlomo's house to be the wedding chamber where he and Shira will spend seven days. It is tradition that the groom goes to retrieve his bride in the evening hours. Barry paces for hours waiting for the sun to relinquish its hold and for darkness to come and for the bride's father to 'approve of the chamber'. Finally, Alon says, "I don't think you'll last much longer, boy. Go get your bride before you burst." Barry takes his few friends that became his attendants and makes his way to Alon's house. Like the parable that Jesus told about the bridesmaids and their oil lamps, Shira is waiting every night, longing to hear Barry's voice. Bracha and the other bridesmaids are also waiting with lamps ready. As Barry approaches Alon's house, he stops outside the courtyard and calls out to Shira. The group waits as Bracha and company come to the gate to let him in. They lead Barry across the short courtyard into the house that he has come to know so well, where Shira is veiled and ready. Then both parties process back to Shlomo's house. Those who hear Barry call out, now stand by the road wishing good fortune to the happy couple as they pass.

As they reach Shlomo's house, Barry and Shira are ushered into the wedding chamber and the door is closed. This is the time when the wedding is 'consummated' and both Bracha and the best man wait outside the room for word that it is 'done'. Barry and Shira stare at each other somewhat awkwardly for a few moments. "Well, this is it, I guess," Barry thinks to himself. After a bit, Shira giggles and grabs Barry's face with her soft hands. They both emit a large sigh and the tension is released.

"I can't believe I'm here," whispers Barry.

"Why? I don't understand?" Shira replies.

"When they dragged me out of that oasis and brought me here, I never thought I'd be as happy as I am at this moment."

"I've dreamed of this moment ever since we returned. Now, we're together forever"

Barry pulls her to him and kisses her. Then Shira looks into Barry's eyes and he can think of nothing else. She touches her hand to the side of his face and kisses him again. The world has passed away and they have only this moment. She starts to remove her dress.

Bracha taps her foot impatiently as an eleven-year-old would. "What is taking so long?" she asks to nobody in particular. "Does it take this long?" she asks of the best man, who is only thirteen, himself. He blushes and shrugs his shoulders. "I want to start celebrating. Don't they know we're waiting? You think that they would have a little compassion for us just standing here." After a half hour, the door cracks open and out steps a weary Barry.

He closes the door softly and says to the two of them, "It is done."

"It's about time," complains Bracha. Barry starts to laugh, which in turn makes the best man laugh. Bracha looks at both of them rather disgustedly at first, but then succumbs to the laughter as well. She goes to hug Barry and he drops to one knee to be closer to her height. She hugs him and says, "I'm glad you are my brother."

"And I'm glad to have you as a sister," Barry responds. "Now, go tell the guests so that they can begin the celebration."

The two run off into the next room and there is quickly a cheer that rises to the heavens. Barry stands up and thinks to himself, "I finally have everything that fame and wealth would have never brought me. I am at peace, maybe for the first time in my life. To think as I was walking across the stage to get my doctorate, that I would be content as a 'pot-patching' blacksmith... scratching out a living in the most primitive conditions... I'm not in Kansas anymore, that's for sure." Barry cracks the door open and goes back into the wedding chamber and, from the front room, another of many cheers is once again hoisted to the heavens.

TIME TO LEAVE

Barry and Shira spend seven days and nights 'knowing each other'. Their food is brought to them and the time becomes a blur as they talk and make plans and love and sleep. After that period, they finally emerge to join the celebration. There is a feast and joy abounds. But soon it is time for them to leave. As a present, Shlomo gives them his small wagon and Ruffy. He is getting too old and doesn't need them as he used to and it will make their journey easier. Barry and Shira load up what few possessions they have and are ready to depart. At first, Shira was happy to follow Barry anywhere. But now as it comes to that time, Shira finds it difficult to go. She hugs each member of her family and tears flow. Barry thanks Alon for everything. Then the two of them climb up into the wagon and Barry bids one last farewell with the promise that they will return as soon as possible.

Barry urges the little donkey forward. Shira turns to look back and waves at the family as they wave goodbye. Once they are down the road and turn the corner, her vision is blocked and Shira turns back around and snuggles close to Barry. "Don't worry, Shira. You will see them again soon."

"I've never been outside the city, except that one time when we were both healed."

"Trust in God. He will see us through."

"You are my husband now. I will trust in you." Shira grabs hold of Barry's arm and lays her head on his shoulder as the wagon bumps along.

Barry decides to go back to the city where they were healed and begin the search there. He finds that Jesus was last reported in the city of Ephraim, north of where they are, and so they begin the trek in search of Jesus. When they arrive in Ephraim, Barry questions all the merchants along the road. Many have no idea who Jesus is, some have heard of his name in story and rumors. But many remember the guy who came to town and drew crowds to hear him speak, even if they didn't know his name. They may be about a month behind him or more. It is hard to tell from all the sketchy and contradicting information Barry hears. They continue north towards Galilee.

With every town, they seem to be closer and the information seems to be less contradicting. Everywhere they go, they find someone who will put them up for the night. Shira helps with the chores before they leave and Barry occasionally has an opportunity to do 'man's work' to help out as well. In one town, a widow put them up and they stayed two nights while Barry fixed part of her house. As they reach Nain, Barry learns that Jesus was up around the Sea of Galilee, but has now crossed the Jordan River and is headed west. Barry is now only about a week behind him. With every town, they get closer. They cross over the river Jordan and reach a city where Jesus was for several days and just left the day before. They spend the night there and Barry is hopeful that they will be able to close in on him in the morning.

Barry has avoided talking to Shira about Jesus because he wouldn't be able to explain to her how he knows all he knows. But now that they are getting close, she presses him for more. That night as they lay in bed, Shira snuggles close and Barry envelopes her in his arms.

"You really believe this man is the Messiah?" Shira asks.

"I know that he is the Messiah," Barry says confidently.

"So, where are his armies? His chariots? He walks the roads like a common man. When will he free us?"

"He will. Just not the way people think."

"How do you know that?"

"When he healed me, he changed my whole mind. Like how I could speak - I can't explain to you how I know what I know. But it will happen."

"I still don't understand why we must follow after him. After we find him, we can go home again?"

"I don't know."

"I miss my family. I don't understand why all of this is so important."

"I know. I miss them too. Just have faith."

"I have faith in God. And in you. I don't think I have very much faith in this man you think is the Messiah."

"Someday you will... someday you will."

The next morning, Barry and Shira set out after breakfast and cleanup are done. As they pass people on the road, all of them have a story of passing a man followed by a crowd. Barry knows they are close. By mid-day, Barry can see a crowd gathered up ahead just outside a small village. He slows the wagon and wanders up to the crowd sitting on the ground and eating lunch. And in the midst of them, Jesus is speaking. Barry stops the wagon and helps Shira down. He grabs some food from the wagon and sits down at the edge of the crowd to listen. As he sits, Jesus again looks straight at him and Barry knows that Jesus is aware of his presence. As Jesus speaks, Barry can see that Shira is listening intently. At some point, Barry too is entranced. He speaks of love and kindness and God and how we are to treat one another. In spite of his very average appearance, his words carry great power and command attention. Soon, Jesus finishes talking and the crowd is breaking up. Barry puts Shira back on the wagon along with another woman who seems to be labored in her walking. She and Shira talk while Barry walks along the road, leading Ruffy and talking to those disciples following Jesus.

That evening, Barry finds a place for them to stay. As Shira strokes her gentle hand across Barry's chest, she asks, "Why did you not talk to Jesus today?"

"I don't know," Barry says as he stares at the ceiling. I finally found him and I was afraid to talk to him."

"Afraid? Why?"

"I don't know. Maybe because I know him for who he truly is."

"I don't understand."

Barry rolls over and puts his hand on her creamy cheek. "I'll talk to him tomorrow. I promise." He gives her a gentle kiss.

"And then we can go home?" Shira coos in an excited tone. Barry gives her a stare and she says, "Well, it can't hurt to ask..." Then she turns over and pulls the covers up tight. Barry sighs.

The next morning, Barry is up early and he's determined to speak to Jesus today. They are now part of the group that leaves and is back on the road. The group is fairly large as there are between eighty and one hundred men at any one time that follow behind Jesus. They walk, talk with each other, ask questions and even tell stories. Jesus even tells a funny story that morning that has everyone laughing. Most follow for a day or two and then return to their home while others from villages ahead join the crowd. There are also women and children in the crowd, some riding in small wagons trailed by goats. On this morning, Barry gets to speak with Matthew and he is amazed at Barry's understanding of what Jesus has said. At the same time, Barry is fascinated by all of Matthew's stories which never make it to the Gospel in written form. Many of the stories reflect the human side of Jesus as he laughed and mourned along with everyone else. Barry begins to see Jesus as a man and it quells some of his anxiety.

After a mid-day break, Barry goes to Jesus as the crowd prepares to depart. As he approaches, Jesus turns to face him and now Barry is finally face to face with Jesus - again. That air of calm that Barry felt when he was changed returns and he feels at ease. Barry clears his throat and says, "I don't know what you did to me. I could never explain it. But I didn't get a chance to thank you, so... thank you."

"What did you do that day?" asks Jesus. "After I left."

"I danced," Barry chuckles. "I ran and jumped and danced and told everyone I saw what happened."

"And who did you say I was?"

"I told everyone that you are the Messiah and that I was a miracle."

"No better thanks could I ask for than that." Jesus turns to walk away and then turns back. He puts his hand on Barry's shoulder and says, "The time is approaching. I am going to Jerusalem for the last time. You are the only one who truly understands the task ahead of me. Do not go far from me, for you have a part to play in my Father's plan."

The crowd is starting to move now and Jesus turns and walks away. Barry stands frozen with Jesus' words ringing in his ears. "Part of the plan? Me? What part? Did he mean an integral part? No, I'm not part of the story... am I? No, I can't be. How could I be? I'm not really even supposed to be here." Barry remembers Shira and snaps out of his thoughts. He goes and gets Shira and the wagon and joins the group as they continue down the road. But Barry talks to only a few of the disciples that afternoon as he wrestles with what Jesus said. That evening, he is still distracted as Shira serves the meal.

"Do you not want to eat?" Shira asks.

"I'm sorry, I was lost in thought. Jesus told me that I'm part of the plan," Barry mumbles.

"What plan? You spoke to him today, can we now go home?"

"No. I must stay with him."

Shira bangs Barry's cup which she is bringing to him on the table. "What is this man to us?" she asks angrily. She sits down across from Barry with her back to him. Barry gets up and walks around to Shira. He kneels down and reaches to move a small wisp of hair from her face.

"We owe him our lives. If it were not for him, you would be dead," Barry says softly. Then stroking her face, he adds with a smile, "And my heart would have died as well."

Shira's eyes tear and she pulls Barry near to her as she hugs his neck. "I'm sorry. I am not being a good wife."

"I could not ask for a better wife."

"All those things he says... I want to believe," Shira says as she pulls away to look into Barry's eyes. "I want to believe like you do. I will do what must be done," she sniffs and uses her apron to dry her eyes. "We will follow him for a long as it takes."

Barry pulls her to himself once more. "I know you didn't ask for this, and I'm sorry. But I love you more than life and it gives me strength when you're near."

After a few moments, Shira shoos him away saying, "Go... eat you supper before it gets cold. Otherwise, God will think I'm a bad wife, even if you don't."

A few weeks later, the crowd arrives in Jerusalem. Jesus stops in Bethany, at the home of Lazarus, as it was written. Barry and Shira push onto Jerusalem and find a place in an inn there. It is the end of Sabbath and everyone in the inn gathers together to talk and to eat. Barry knows that tomorrow is Palm Sunday, although he is the only one in the world that knows it by that name. This is the beginning of the trip to the cross for Jesus. Being out on the road, it is easy for Barry to get caught up in the conversations and questions. Now that they are in Jerusalem, Barry is now faced with the reality that the man he's come to know will be dead within the week. That night Barry sits on the edge of the bed. Shira tries to divert his attention, but her gentle ways are of no comfort to Barry tonight. As she sleeps, comfortably unaware of the upcoming events, Barry's thoughts haunt him.

"I had so little time. All the things I wanted to know, so many questions I never got a chance to ask. I can't believe I'm here and all I can do is watch now. And how do I figure into this? What am I supposed to do? I can't stop this, can I? Is there something that I'm supposed to alter? Jesus said I was part of this story, but what part? I got everything that I'd ask God for and now I'm sorry I asked. I'm not sure I can watch this happen. It might have been better if I had never found Jesus. I'd still be living in peaceful bliss with my lovely wife. Perhaps we should go back to Timnah, like Shira wants. What good can I do here? And yet, Jesus told me to stay, so I have to stay. I don't have a choice. But what will I do?" Barry ponders his fate and that of his friend until sleep is unavoidable and drags him into a deep slumber.

THE BEGINNING OF THE END

Barry is up early, despite his lack of sleep. He wakes Shira and they get an early start so that they will be there when Jesus enters the city. Barry drags Shira out to the main street as she asks, "Why are we coming here? How do you know he will be here today?"

"He will be. Let's go over there. There will be shade there until he comes." Barry says in a very boyish tone.

"It's too early. Nobody is coming this early." Shira complains.

"I want to get the good seats."

"Good seat? I don't understand. What is so good about sitting?"

"Oh, ah... never mind," Barry says realizing his brain had slipped into his old time.

The shadows are cast long as the sun begins its climb into the cloudless sky. Shira sits with her arms crossed and complaining that her work is not getting done. Barry tries to cajole her and knows that the crowds will start to gather any time now. Minutes pass into hours. Shira finally loses her patients, tells Barry she will be back if anything happens and marches back towards the inn. Barry sits and watches the people walking back and forth. More hours pass and Barry begins to doubt. "Maybe this is the wrong day. Well, now that I think of it, I can't remember if the story actually said 'morning'..."

Just before mid-day, Shira comes walking out to where Barry is sitting and looking very bored. She has a very convicting look on her face and Barry looks at her very sheepishly. "Are you going to come in and eat?" Shira asks in a condescending voice. But she is cut short by a voice that cries out, "He is coming!" Before Barry can say anything, people start to scurry in every direction. There is suddenly a cacophony of cries, "He is here!", "It's the man they call the Messiah!", "He's the new king!" There are some who run to the road with palm branches and lay them in the dirt. Others are taking the clothes off their backs and throwing them into the road. Barry is frozen in amazement. Once again, he is watching the Bible come to life before his very eyes. There is yelling and cheering as Jesus comes through the gate. As he rides by, the crowds converge behind him like water flowing into a void left by his passing. There are some Roman guards nearby and officers on horses who talk among themselves, but seem neither impressed nor concerned as the celebration continues towards the temple. Barry pulls Shira to him and they blend into the processional.

Before the crowd settles at the temple courtyard and Jesus begins to speak, several blind people and those with deformities are led into the courtyard. One of them is a young girl, about thirteen, and is lying on a litter. She has a high fever and is unconscious. Barry and Shira walk past her to find a place to sit. As they pass, Shira comes close and wraps her arms around one of Barry's arms and clutches it to her tightly. Jesus comes into the courtyard and begins to heal them by laying his hand on them. With each miracle, there is a gasp from the crowd. As he comes to the girl, her father is crying and says to Jesus. "Please, rabbi, heal my daughter. She is my only child and her mother is dead. It is said you can heal her and I believe you to be merciful."

Jesus slowly walks over to her and kneels down. He looks at her for a small time and then places his hand on her head. After a few seconds, she opens her eyes and there is another great collective gasp from the crowd. The father is speechless. After Jesus stands up, the girl slowly sits up and looks around. "Papa!" she yells as she springs from the litter and runs to hug the father.

"Thank you. What is mine is yours. Simply ask," the man pleads.

"It is your faith that has healed your daughter," Jesus replies. He turns to the crowd and says, "The key to my Father's kingdom is your faith."

He begins to address the crowd as the father sits with the daughter clutched tightly in his arms to listen. After Jesus speaks, Shira excuses herself from Barry as he talks with the other men. That night, it is Shira that sits at the edge of the bed staring into space. "What's the matter?" Barry asks.

"That girl today... that was me... wasn't it?" Shira says in a very detached tone.

"Yes. Yes it was," Barry responds sitting next to her and putting his arm around her.

"I never understood... until today. You said I would understand someday. I looked into that father's eyes. I saw the fear my father must have felt. I saw the smile on the girl's face. I talked to her afterwards. The last thing she remembered before she got sick was being in trouble. She said that now she has a chance to make it right."

Barry gives Shira a squeeze and says, "And she'll probably make some lucky boy a fine wife."

Shira looks up at Barry and says, "I do believe. Although, I don't understand everything he said, I will trust in him and believe."

The next day, Shira insists that Barry go alone today and that she must catch up on her work. Barry sits in the inner court with the rest of the men as Jesus begins to speak. Barry begins to look around and notices that not all those who have come are intent on listening. Barry watches the Pharisees who have come as they whisper among themselves. They are already hatching their plans. Barry knows what they're up to and so does Jesus. He throws an occasional glance at them as he speaks. Barry is still concerned about his part in all of this. He still can't figure out what he is supposed to do.

That evening, he arrives back to the inn to a loving hug and a hot meal. Shira asks about the day's events. Barry says nothing concerning the plots of the Pharisees. Shira would not understand and he would be hard pressed to explain how he knows these things. The next two days he tries to speak with some of the twelve, but they are still clueless to the coming events. Most of them are just glad to be back in Jerusalem and off the road and pass Barry off as a worrier. It is the evening before Passover. Shira is trying to discuss Passover plans with Barry, but he is distracted. He knows that tomorrow evening is the last. His mind races with all sorts of wild ideas and trying to figure out what he's supposed to be doing.

The next evening, those staying at the inn, gather to celebrate the Passover. Barry grows restless as the minutes tick away in his mind. This is the night and he still hasn't figured out what his part in this story will be. "Wait a minute," Barry thinks as his epiphany dawns, "I don't have to figure out my part. Jesus already knows what my part will be, or else he wouldn't have said I had one. I need to talk to Jesus. But, this is the night. He's in that upper room right now telling his disciples to eat from the bread and to drink of the wine. I can't just go breaking in on that and say, 'Hey, can we talk about me here?' But I've got to talk to him tonight." Barry puts his arm around Shira and pulls her close. He whispers into her ear, "I have to leave." and he kisses her on the side of the head and turns to go.

"Go? Now?" Shira whispers as she grabs his sleeve and attempts to pull him back. "Where would you go tonight? It's Passover."

"I know," Barry says gently removing her hand from his sleeve. "I'll be back soon."

The air is brisk but there is no wind. The night is silent and the moon shrouds the town in an innocent dream of shadows. "I have no idea where he is now exactly," Barry reasons as he slides through the moonlight, "but I know where he will be eventually. He goes to the garden tonight to pray. I'll talk to him there after the disciples fall asleep." Barry makes his way outside the walls and to the garden of Gethsemane. He finds a grove of olive trees standing like old crouched men in the darkness. This is where Jesus has come on a couple of occasions after he had preached in the city. There are some large rocks and a stand to hold a torch. An extinguished torch sets in the stand, silently awaiting its visitors who would be coming soon. Barry finds a place of cover near the clearing and hides himself from view. The time passes so slowly that Barry can't concentrate on anything. His mind is a blur of so many different thoughts. The wind picks up and the old crouched men start to sway in shadow ever so slowly.

In the distance, a couple of lights appear. "It's them," Barry whispers. The lights seem to hover motionless now.

But Barry can hear the rustle of feet along the garden path in the distance. The ghostly glow of figures can now be seen and Barry grows anxious. Soon, Jesus appears and is followed by Peter, James and John. They come to a stop next to the old torch. Peter removes the old torch and replaces it with one of the two torches they have with them. Barry strains to hear the conversation. Jesus takes the other torch from John and says to them, "I am going on a little further. Sit here, keep watch and pray that you may be strong in the times to come."

"Why not just pray here, master?" asked Peter.

"I will be tempted here tonight. I would not have your words weaken my heart," Jesus says and turns and walks further into the garden. The disciples find places to sit against the rocks. They are already yawning and stretching.

"I ate too much," James complains. "I'm ready for sleep."

"You always eat too much. Why do we come all the way out here tonight?" asks John.

"And what was all that talk about betrayal?" asks James.

"Judas left early. What was that all about?" mused Peter.

"He had something for Judas to do. He told him to be quick about it too. Like Judas would ever be quick at anything," James quipped. They all chuckled.

"Still, he seems more troubled than usual," says Peter.

"It's all the traveling. Give him another day or two and he'll be fine." says James. "I know I'll be glad if we stay here another two weeks. I like being in the city better than traveling out on the dusty roads."

A quiet comes over them as they look around and stare into the darkness. Their eyes being to become heavy and some of their heads begin to nod. Suddenly, there is a light that appears and Jesus returns to the clearing. "Wake up!" Jesus commands. All three of their heads pop awake.

"Please, stay awake and pray with me." His voice is as Barry has never heard before. There is a fear in his tone. There is an uncertainty in his glances that seem so out of place. He turns with a blank stare and staggers into the garden again.

"We must stay awake and pray," Peter says. He rubs his face in an attempt to become more lucid. But his words are already falling on deaf ears as James and John are already nodding off again. Peter makes a noble effort to try and keep himself awake. "Go to sleep, Peter," Barry says in his head. "You're supposed to go to sleep again... Will you go to sleep... you're wasting my opportunity... go to sleep!"

Finally, Peter drifts off to sleep. Barry knows that it is now or never. He gathers his courage and sneaks past the disciples in the direction that Jesus had gone. He gets to a spot where he can see the dimly lit torch of Jesus. Barry stops near an empty torch stand and is frozen in his tracks. "The final prayers of Jesus," Barry thinks. "I can't interrupt him. Maybe I should just wait here. But I've got to talk to him... No, I'll just wait." Barry stands debating with himself when Jesus walks back to where he is.

"Jesus!" exclaims Barry.

"You've come to me in this hour," Jesus utters as he places his torch in the empty stand.

"I had to. You told me I had a part to play, but I don't know what it is."

Jesus places his hand on Barry's shoulder. "Time is short, so listen to me. The betrayer comes and my time is at hand."

Barry tries to hold back the tears, but the humanity of the moment takes hold and he begins to cry, "I know. But why this covenant? Why can't you just stay a little longer?"

Jesus shoves Barry back. "Away from me Satan, I will not be tempted here," Jesus decries. "Do not tempt me here!"

"I'm sorry," Barry cries uncontrollably. "I know what you must do. Ask me, and I will stand with you. Even to death." Barry tries to compose himself and wipes the tears from his face.

Jesus once more grabs Barry by the shoulder and says, "This cup is mine alone to drink from. But you show great faith for you have now seen me. Now, I need your faith for when I am gone."

"Ok," Barry sniffs, still wiping away his tears, "what must I do?"

"My Father in heaven has sent his word through the prophets, but kingdoms still come and go. All the power of this earth is fleeting and the people forget the words of men alone. I make a covenant that will last the age until my Father makes it all new. I am changing your name. From now on, you will be known as Matthias, 'Gift of God'."

"Matthias? You mean the one who replaces Judas?"

"Yes. Stay close to the eleven after it is done. They are still weak for they do not know what is about to happen. They will need your strength. They can use your witness. You will take your place among the disciples and be to them a small voice to start them on their journey."

"I will do that for you, my savior."

Jesus smiles ever so slightly as Barry utters that title. He places his hands on either side of Barry's face and kisses Barry's forehead. Jesus' head then whips around as if there had been a loud noise, but Barry hears nothing. "Now go," whispers Jesus, "for the betrayer is here and there is no more time." Jesus takes the torch and turns to leave. Barry stands frozen once again, watching his best friend walk to his death. As the darkness closes in and Barry is left in the moonlight, his strength fails and he drops to his knees. He begins to cry again.

Soon, another source of strength takes hold of Barry and he gets up and runs to the clearing. He stops short of the light and crouches down to watch. Jesus is scolding Peter, James and John asking why they sleep, but they still don't understand. Barry can see a line of torches making its way to the clearing. Judas comes in ahead of them with the rest of the disciples. As they enter the light of the torches, the other James says, "Soldiers are coming, Master." A chorus of 'What do we do?' breaks out among the disciples, but Jesus raises his hand and quiets them. He hands the torch to John as Judas approaches. Judas moves to Jesus' side and leans in to kiss Jesus on the cheek. He continues past Jesus to stand behind him. Jesus' gaze remains straight ahead on the approaching soldiers, but he says, "You would betray me with a kiss, Judas?"

As the disciples begin to ask, 'What is happening?', 'What did you do?', 'Who are they coming for?' Jesus once again holds up his hands and quiets them. Soon, the soldiers reach the garden and stop and a larger crowd follows behind them and stops short of the light. There is an eerie silence and then the soldier in charge points at Jesus and demands, "Arrest this one." As one of the soldiers steps forward and begins to draw his sword, Peter draws a short sword from a sheath strapped to his waist and swings at the soldier. Peter is not very skilled with a sword and the soldier easily blocks the wild swing with his shield. But, it is so wild, that the sword bounces off the shield and slaps the soldier on the side of the head as he had no helmet. When the sword falls, it takes off part of the soldier's ear.

Jesus jumps between Peter and the soldier and yells, "Stop!" Jesus picks up the piece of the ear and says to the disciples, "Have you heard nothing that I have said to you? Those who live by the sword, die by the sword. This is not the way of my father." Jesus walks to the soldier and moves the soldier's hand away from the side of his head where he was trying to stop the bleeding. Jesus places his hand with the ear up to the side of the soldier's head. Within seconds, the ear is healed and Jesus steps away. The soldiers stand in amazement as the one soldier tugs at his ear. The soldier in charge examines the ear and, except for the blood that remains, can see no sign of it being cut. There are mummers from the crowd standing just outside the light of the torches.

"Am I leading a rebellion," Jesus shouts to the crowd in the shadows, "that you have come with swords and clubs? Every day I was with you in the temple courts, and you did not lay a hand on me. This is your hour, when darkness reigns." Then turning to his disciples he says, "This is the way it must be. This is what was written."

"Arrest him," the soldier in charge says in a soft voice.

"Sir? My ear... is he not who they say he is?" the soldier who's ear had been cut asks.

"I know," the soldier in charge says apologetically, "but I have my orders. Arrest him!" He approaches Jesus as they are binding Jesus' hands and says, "If you are the son of this Hebrew god, then I'm sorry. Forgive me." He then turns to the disciples and says, "Leave. Leave now... save yourselves before it is too late."

There are loud protests from the crowd in the shadows when the soldier dismisses the disciples. The soldier turns to address the crowd. "Silence!" the soldier demands. "My orders are clear. I need only to arrest this man." The disciples are still unmoved in shock. Once again the solider orders, "I said leave now, before I change my mind!" This time the disciples turn and flee into the night. The soldiers form rank and escorts Jesus away. Barry watches them snake into the distance as the line of torches slowly disappears. After a short time, Peter comes running back through the area heading in the direction that Jesus had been taken.

Barry remains motionless for a while. Then he stands up, still in shock. His mind is in a haze. He begins to slowly walk, but is not aware that he is walking nor of where he is going. He feels numb all over. "It's done. He's gone. Just like that. Tomorrow, he will die and there is nothing anyone can do. He has to; otherwise, he can't save us. But I already miss him. Matthias? He called me Matthias? I'm to join the eleven? How can this be when Matthias already appeared in my Bible? Was I... am I the original Matthias? Have I always been Matthias, stuck in this weird loop of time? Mother said I had a special purpose... did she know?" Barry continues to wander through the garden aimlessly and muttering to himself.

THE WAIT

Barry wanders through the night, his mind lost in deep thought. His gate is now more of a slow stagger as his strength is waning from lack of sleep. His body and mind are still numb. His contemplation is broken only by the dawn as the sun begins to return to the sky. "It's morning?" Barry asks astonished. "Have I been walking all night? I've got to get back to Shira. All the disciples will begin to panic today. I must be careful..." Barry hears a creaking sound off to his left. Panicked, he whips around to see a body. It is Judas hanging from a tree; the pail he stood on not far from his feet. The rope creaks in the crook of the branches as the breeze moves him back and forth. A true fear pervades Barry now and goes down to his bones. "I've got to get to back to Shira!" Barry races for the inn using what little strength he has left and as fast as his feet will take him.

Barry stumbles in the door and closes it behind him as he pants and puffs. Shira stands up with a squeal from the end of the bed where she has been sitting and crying. The two of them fall in each other's arms. Barry holds her tight as his upper body heaves up and down trying to breathe.

Shira buries her face in him as her tears are a mix of joy and concern. "I didn't know where you were," Shira says hysterically with her head still buried. "Some of the women this morning are saying that Jesus and his disciples were arrested and killed. I thought you were..."

"No. I'm alright," Barry consoles her as his breath is returning. "They just arrested Jesus. The disciples escaped." Barry feels his legs about to collapse. He leads her to the edge of the bed and they both sit, still clinging to each other.

"Is Jesus dead?"

"No. Not yet. But they will crucify him today."

"Crucify him? Why? What has he done?"

"Nothing. It is the Pharisees... It is the Sanhedrin. They will accuse him of heresy and will have Pilot send him to his death."

"How do you know this? How do you know that it will happen that way?"

"Because it was written that way. He is fulfilling the words of Isaiah. And there is nothing we can do."

"I'm so scared. I don't want to lose you."

"There's more. You must hear it. Jesus changed my name. He said I am now Matthias."

"Matthias? What does he want from you?"

"He wants me to become one of the twelve disciples, to replace Judas."

"Replace? Was he arrested with Jesus?"

"No. He betrayed Jesus. He hung himself outside town."

"I'm confused. It makes no sense. None of this makes any sense."

Barry caresses her head to his chest and says, "Don't worry about it now. Just breathe." He pulls her down with him as he lies down on the bed. Shira sobs as Barry stares at the ceiling and they continue to cling to each other. Both of them are exhausted and they both eventually drift off to sleep.

There is a loud noise, like something dropped, outside the door followed by a woman's voice. Barry shoots straight up in the bed, waking Shira. Barry looks around the room and tries to clear the haze in his head.

"What is wrong, Oded?" Shira asks.

"What time is it?" Barry asks looking for the sun coming through the shutters. But there is no sun. It is not night, but there is little light to illuminate the darkened room. Shira gets up from the bed to light an oil lamp. Barry jumps up from the bed and exclaims, "I've missed it!"

"Missed what?" Shira asks. Barry stumbles to the door as his legs were hanging over the bed and are still slightly numb. "Don't leave me again, please?" begs Shira.

Barry comes back and hugs her. "I have to go, but I'll be back before evening. I promise! Don't be afraid." He kisses her and runs from the room. Outside the inn, he runs to the edge of town, outside the walls, and makes his way to Golgotha. He climbs the hill not knowing what he will see and not knowing if he wants to see. It is overcast and the wind is picking up. A clap of thunder sounds like a canon and the lightning flashes. When he finally arrives, he stops and is devastated. He slowly walks to the small crowd standing in front of the cross. Mary, his mother, is there, as is Peter, Matthew and Mary Magdalene. There are some in the crowd that Barry recognizes as 'occasional' followers who came and went from the throng that followed Jesus. It begins to rain. The Roman soldiers begin to scramble for cover and the crowd starts to disperse. Barry lifts his eyes to the cross. His stomach starts to churn as he sees the extensive disfiguration done to Jesus' face and body. It is as nothing that Barry could have ever imagined. The pain of Barry's grief begins to choke his throat. Tears well up in his eyes even as his mind is numb, overwhelmed in the spectacle.

Jesus is dead. The attendants are already beginning to take down the cross. As they lower it to the ground, Jesus' limp body sags to and fro as gravity tugs at it. His limbs are ripped from the nails and his body is covered with a cloth. The lightning flashes and the thunder peals once again. One of the men standing in front begins to direct those wrapping up Jesus and they begin to carry him off. Barry follows behind the small crowd. Peter embraces him as they walk. Peter tries to tell Barry several times of his own denial, but the grief chokes his speech each time. They reach the tomb and Barry and Peter help roll the stone open at the entrance. The men carrying Jesus take him inside and the stone is rolled back. The women discuss coming back to finish preparing the body after the Sabbath. Peter and Barry walk back to town as the small crowd mills about the tomb.

Once again, Peter begins to explain what happen that night. "You denied him," says Barry.

"Yes," Peter says ashamed with his head hanging down.

"Three times... Before the cock crowed," continues Barry. Peter stops and his eyes grow big and he stares at Barry.

"How did you know that?" Peter asks in amazement.

"Because Jesus told you that you would."

"But you were not there."

"Jesus told it to me. He changed my name like he changed yours. He called me Matthias."

"Why?" Peter begged.

"I don't know," Barry lies. "But Jesus is not gone. We will see him again."

"No! No! He's dead!" Peter says angrily. "And we're next!"

"It won't happen like that," Barry tries to explain. "He told us he would return, don't you remember. We will see him again."

"We must hide," Peter says not listening to Barry. "No! We must leave this place while we still can. The disciples have a place. I will take you there," Peter says in a panicked tone.

"No. Listen to me... Go be with the others. But just be patient. Tell them they must be patient – they must wait," Barry says reassuringly.

Peter stares at him a second, trying to believe. Then he turns to leave with the parting remark, "We are all dead men." Barry stands and watches him disappear in the rain.

Barry comes in the door completely soaked. "Where have you been?" Shira asks concerned. "Have you just been standing out in the rain?" she says in a condescending tone.

"Actually, I have," Barry says.

"Well get out of those wet clothes before you get sick." She goes to touch him and then changes her mind and says, "And quit dripping on the floor."

Barry changes clothes and tells Shira what he saw. She is quite moved but tries her best to continue to be supportive. They go to the main room to eat and to begin the Sabbath. There are several comments about the day's happenings. Most people are unsure of what they have seen and don't understand it any more than Shira does. It is a quiet evening. The rain has finally stopped and the air is still. The shock is starting to pass and now Barry looks to the future. He is the only one in the whole world that knows what is truly about to happen. As he and Shira settle in to go to sleep, he thinks about the events he has put her through. "She didn't ask for this kind of life," Barry thinks as he cuddles her close, "but she's been my support in these difficult times. Even though we've been married for such a short time, I don't know how I would cope without her. I'm finding it harder to imagine my old life anymore. It is with her that I feel complete." As the lamp is blown out and Barry heaves a big sigh, he thinks, "Gee... I wish I could be there to see the big event... oh, *maybe I can...*"

THE BIG EVENT

The sun sifting through the small slits in the closed shutters the next morning finds Barry and Shira still in bed. Shira is ready to get up as duty demands, but Barry pulls her back into bed and they spend the morning in quiet reflection of what all has flooded into their lives since they had met one another. Later, Shira is tending to her Sabbath tasks but Barry keeps getting underfoot. She attempts to shoo him out of the room, but he is deep in planning. Shira has no idea what he is planning, but she already doesn't like it. "What are you going to do now?" she asks.

"Nothing. What are you doing?" Barry asks without making eye contact.

"Nothing? Then we're free to go home. I'll pack starting tonight," she responds.

"No. We can't leave yet."

"Then tell me what you're planning."

"We should get you a new apron," Barry says as he tries to hug her.

"Oded!"

Barry sighs heavily, "I'm going out tonight. I didn't want you to worry."

"Tonight? Where are you going this time?"

"There's something I have to see... if it's possible. I can't explain it... it's just something I have to do." Barry puts his arms around her and softly says, "Trust me. I won't do anything dangerous."

"How many times have I heard that?"

As everyone is retiring to their rooms after dinner, Barry finalizes his plans. He slips out close to midnight and heads for the tomb. He doesn't know what to expect. At first, he believes that it may be a glorious event. Then he begins to think that he may not see anything and it may all be a waste of time. In the end, Barry is willing to take the chance to see one of the greatest events in all of heaven and earth.

Barry arrives in the garden next to the tomb. There are four Roman soldiers standing guard. Barry finds a place concealed from the sight of the soldiers and settles down to wait. It's a cool but pleasant night. The air is still so he takes precautions to be extra quiet. Barry is excited, although in the back of his mind he knows he may be disappointed. The hours drag on and Barry fights to stay awake. Then his head snaps up when he hears a noise. He had nodded off to sleep, but now the guards are changing. Barry figures it must be two or three in the morning. He takes advantage of all the noise of clanking armor to stretch and yawn before settling back in. As much as he fights it, Barry nods back off to sleep, although it is a light sleep.

He is awakened when one of the guards starts to walk about. As he gathers himself, Barry watches as the guards are restless and are yawning and stretching. "My Latin is a little rusty and I'm not sure that's pure Latin, but it sounds like their complaining about being here," Barry muses to himself. "I guess I don't blame them. Who wants to stand guard in the middle of the night over a dead Jew? They have no idea." Suddenly, there is a rush of a warm wind with a force that knocks Barry over and accompanied by a loud crackling noise. The guards with their shields are fighting against the wind and wondering what is going on. As Barry flops over and starts to get back up, he glances up into the sky and there they are. It begins as a small bluish-white light, but in a short amount of time, it moves to the ground like a meteorite and Barry can see them as they land. "Whoa," Barry exclaims trying to remember to be quiet, "I see angels!"

It's dawn when Barry arrives back at the room. Shira is stirring as Barry tries to quietly come in the door, but he wakes her up. Barry lights a lamp and sits on the edge of the bed next to Shira. Shira turns and sits up in the bed. She looks at Barry and gasps, "What happened to your face?"

"What's wrong with my face?" Barry asks in an excited voice.

"It looks like it's burned. It's all red. Does it hurt?" she asks as she tenderly touches the skin.

"No," Barry says as he feels of his face.

"Where did you go?" Shira asks.

"I went to the tomb of Jesus. He's back. He has been resurrected!"

"What? Oded, you've been dreaming," Shira says as she starts to get out of bed.

"Does this look like I've been dreaming?" Barry asks, referring to his face, as he grabs her and sits her back on the bed.

"So, where did you go? What did you see?" Shira asks as the excitement is rising in her voice.

"I was sitting in the garden, across from the tomb. It was about an hour or two before dawn, I guess. Suddenly, there was a great wind that knocked me over. It was warm and dry and made me all tingly, don't ask me why. And I heard this noise. As I was getting up, I saw them! Angels! They shot to the ground like lightning. There were eleven of them. They all glowed with a bluish white light. But it wasn't a radiant light..."

"Radiant?" Shira struggles with the word.

Barry then realizes that the language itself doesn't have words to describe what he has seen. "They didn't shine bright like a lamp," Barry struggles, "the light was part of their skin. Seven of them were like soldiers. They wore what looked like armor, like what the Roman guards were wearing, but it wasn't separate on the outside. It glowed too and it looked like part of their skin - like one piece of clay that was molded into a solid figure. And they had short, stubby wings on their back." Barry gets up and gets some water to drink and then sits back down. "They landed on all sides of the guards. They carried spears which looked like they were made of gold, but they glowed too. One of the Romans drew their sword like he was going to fight them. One angel just pointed its spear at the guard and the guard went to the ground. I don't know if he was dead. The rest of the guards dropped their shield and weapons and ran off at that point. I forgot myself and I laughed out loud. They heard me and one of them turned to look at me and I thought I was a dead man."

Shira grabs his arm and appears to be frightened as well. Barry reassures her, "I'm fine, but I began to think that maybe you had been right and I should not have gone." Shira gives him a look of 'I told you so'. "The one looking at me then jumped straight up into the air maybe sixty feet or so..."

"Feet?" Shira asks again.

"Oh. Ah… six or seven reeds high." Shira's eyes opened wide. Barry continues, "And it is coming down right on top of me. I fell down, face first, to the ground and its spear came to rest on the back of my neck. It was sharp, and it felt like a normal blade. I looked at its feet."

"His feet?" Shira interrupted.

"I'm not sure. They had strange faces and slender, straight bodies. They really didn't look like man or woman. Their hair was straight and didn't come to their shoulders and they had very plain faces. Maybe that is what happened to my face - when I was close to its feet, I felt the glow on my face. I slowly turned my head to look up at it and it just stared at me. But after a bit, it moved the spear and I was able to rise up and get a better look. It never said a word, but it leapt up into the sky with the other six and was gone as fast as it came. Three of the four remaining looked like beautiful women, with big dresses and long flowing hair. They had large dove-like wings. The last one looked like a bare-chested man, maybe seven foot… I mean… more than a reed tall, with long flowing hair as well. He had giant wings like a barn owl."

"Barn owl?" Shira asked?

"It's a big bird. Never mind that part. He had a giant book in his right hand. After I stood back up and after the soldiers left, I noticed that he was looking at me too. I was so scared; I thought I would soil myself."

Shira laughs a little schoolgirl laugh.

"It wasn't funny," Barry says as he is obviously embarrassed.

"I'm sorry" Shira half-apologizes trying to stifle a giggle.

"Well, I guess you're right. It is pretty funny now. But then he turns away from me towards the tomb. The three women begin to sing. It hurt my ears at first, but then I could hear them inside my head. They were praising God and calling on his powers. Suddenly the stone started rolling away all by itself. The big angel then opened the book and stretched out his huge wings and his glow began to ungulate... uh, that is, his glow got brighter and then softer and then brighter. The inside of the tomb glowed with a bright, white light. It was so bright; it hurt my eyes to look at it. It was like looking at the sun. Someone then began to walk out because I could see the outline as he blocked the light. As the big angel read, the wind began to pick up again and the singing became louder. Soon, it sounded like there were more than just three singing – it sounded like hundreds. As the figure exited the tomb, the light inside was all but blocked by the silhouette. Then the light faded and I could see it was Jesus. He glowed the same way the angels glowed. I was so overjoyed; all I could think to do was run to him. When I came closer, I was blocked by one of the female angels. As she looked at me, I could hear her voice in my head. She told me, 'You cannot see him yet. He is not ready. Go back to Shira and tell her what you have seen. Tell her to look to her dream that she may also have faith.' That's when I left and came back here. What dream?"

Barry looks at Shira and she has lost her smile. "What's wrong?" Barry asks.

"I had a dream," Shira says in a monotone voice as her face takes on a blank stare. "I thought it was just a dream. I was sitting next to Jesus and he was speaking to me. He told me that you had a special task to do and not to be afraid or give up hope. That he was still with us." After a short pause, she looks into Barry's eyes and asks, "What does it mean?"

"It means that I am Matthias. And our lives are no longer our own. I will serve the Lord with all my heart, and with all my soul and with all my strength."

"I will always love you. And I will follow you where ever you go," Shira says as she draws Barry close to her.

"And I will always love you," Barry responds.

As they sit on the bed, clinging tightly to one another, Shira finally breaks the silence. "That female angel that you talked to..." she asks hesitantly.

"Yes?" Barry says softly.

"Was she prettier than me?"

TONGUES OF FLAME

It is well into the morning. Even though he had been up most of the night, Barry is too wired to sleep. The redness of his face subsides in time. He continues to tell Shira all the small details he had left out before as he remembers them. There is a knock at the door. Shira jumps and looks worried at Barry. Barry waves off her panic and says, "Don't be afraid." He opens the door and sees one of the disciples that joined the group just before they reached Jerusalem.

"I come on behalf of those who still follow him," he says.

"You are welcome here," says Barry. "Come in, please."

The man enters the room and greets Shira. He says, "I bring amazing news," he says excitedly, "Jesus has arisen. The disciples are meeting."

"I will be there," Barry says. The disciple seems surprised that Barry takes the news so calmly.

"Good," the disciple says hesitantly, "God be with you." He leaves and Barry closes the door.

"See?" Barry asks Shira as she smiles at him. "What did I tell you?"

Later that afternoon, Barry and Shira go to the upper room where the disciples and some of the families are gathered. Peter relates the story of how Barry had known of Peter's betrayal and of his name being changed to Matthias. Later that evening, Jesus appears to them. The disfigurement that Barry had seen is gone and Jesus looks like the friend Barry knows. Barry concludes that Jesus left the holes in his hands and feet as proof to the other disciples. Jesus also refers to Barry as Matthias throughout the evening. He eats with them and speaks to them about what has happened since he left them. Mostly, Jesus speaks of what will come and keeps reassuring them that all is well for the moment. And then, he tells them he will return and Jesus simply disappears.

The disciples continue to meet every day, talking about what had happened and breaking bread together. Barry tells stories and continues to encourage them not to doubt. He takes it as a personal challenge to convince Thomas to believe before Jesus returns, but he is unsuccessful. It is a busy time as everyone is preparing to travel to the Mount of Olives. Most of the disciples are packing for a week, but Barry tells them to be prepared to be there for forty days. Some heed his words and some do not. Most of the wives and children stay behind as the group travels to the mountain. Shira is one that is staying, as she kisses Barry goodbye and wishes him well.

Jesus comes to the disciples several times to teach and eat with them. Barry summons the courage to speak to Jesus alone as everyone is eating.

"Forgive me, Master," Barry begins sheepishly. "But, I have to ask. What is heaven like? How are you able to be here?"

Amused at the question, Jesus responds, "Why do you ask, Matthias?"

"I'm just curious. I can't discuss this with anybody else. What is heaven? Is it a temporal shift?... Another physical dimension?... A collection of ethereal energy?" Jesus laughs a little laugh. "And you," Barry continues as he pokes at Jesus. "I know the body is so you can relate to us, but you eat? I know it's not necessary... is it? And the angels I saw had that translucent glow and you don't anymore. Is that translucent glow the normal state or is that a temporal thing as well?"

Jesus shakes his head and then smiles as Barry. "This is really eating at you, isn't it?"

"Yes!" Barry quietly exclaims. "You know that. It eats at everybody. Trying to understand something we can't see, can't touch, can't measure and can't prove with any means of science that I'm aware of. I mean, quantum physics is nothing compared to what you did to my brain..." Jesus continues to eat. "And that's just for starters," Barry continues. "What about black holes and evolution and the big bang theory..."

Jesus nods his head as he swallows the last bit of food. "Some things are similar to what you imagine. Most things, however, are still way beyond even your comprehension. You often lament that there are no words in Aramaic, Hebrew or Greek to describe everything that is in your head. You've had to use words from your old life just to ask the questions. So it is with my Father's house. So I also lament that you would not understand even if I could describe it to you... which I can't. For there are no words, not even in your native language." Jesus puts his hand on Barry's shoulder and speaks in a serious tone. "Many men will spend their whole lives trying to prove or disprove the existence of what they cannot understand. All their efforts will have no effect on what actually exists except to blind them to their opportunity to see it. Trust in faith that what you seek, but don't understand, is there and you will see the gates opened before your eyes. Just as those looking for it without faith, but with their own understanding, will be pecking like chickens at the ground unable to look up as the gate hits them in the head and kills them." Jesus bangs the side of his head with his hand. Barry laughs and nods his head. Jesus stands up and says with a smile before he walks away, "Put your life into faith, Matthias. Faith that I know what I'm doing. Faith that my Father knows what he is doing. Everything else will take care of itself."

Soon, the disciples come down from the mountain and Barry arrives at the house of a disciple where Shira is staying. He is not yet to the door when Shira appears and jumps into his arms. "I missed you so much," She says.

"Oh? I didn't miss you at all," Barry says in a very droll voice.

"What?" Shira asks astonished and pulls away from Barry. Barry can't hold back his smile and begins to snicker. "Oh... very funny," Shira says. "Maybe I should let you fix your own supper."

A couple of days later, they meet again in the upper room and Peter addresses the disciples. "Dear brothers," Peter begins, "let me have your attention." He opens a copy of the Septuagint and reads the passage about Judas. He then addresses the disciples again saying, "We need to replace Judas Iscariot as one of the twelve. Who shall we choose?"

"Joseph of Bethany," comes a voice from the back. There is a general murmur among the crowd. James, the brother of Jesus stands and says, "I would choose Matthias of Timnah." Again there is a murmur. Barry knows Joseph and thinks very highly of him, but he also knows the die has already been cast. After some discussion, it comes time to decide.

"Both of these men have a strong witness," Peter states. "How do we choose?"

"We don't choose," Matthew says. "Let God choose whom he will to serve him."

"Yes," says one from the crowd, "cast lots and let God choose."

"Very well," says Peter. "The eleven will cast lots."

After a prayer to God to choose, the eleven cast their lots and they all fall to Barry, as he knew they would. The fact that they all went to him convinces everyone present and there are no arguments. Barry is now one of the twelve apostles. The disciples continue to meet and Barry waits in anticipation every day for Pentecost to come. He already knows what will happen, and finds it hard to not blurt it out to everyone else. Peter sends for representatives from many different areas. Many come, but they are not sure the reason for the gathering. Very few speak Greek and it is difficult to understand everyone. There are several languages that Barry has never heard before.

It is the morning of Pentecost and Barry can hardly contain his emotions. The believers that were sent for now assemble in the usual location. Through the open window comes a rush of warm wind followed by a crackling sound. It catches everyone by surprise and the room quiets. To Barry, it is all too familiar. It is the same breeze he felt and the same noise he heard that night when the angels came to the tomb. The time has arrived.

A wavering beam of light like a really thick laser shoots through the window. As it enters the room, it splits into smaller beams and crisscrosses the room touching most of the men sitting there. The light is only there for a few seconds and then disappears just as quickly as it came. But

PROOF!

it leaves everyone it touches with the same blue-white
iridescent glow that adorned the angels that night at the
tomb. Barry is amazed as he holds up his hand examining
it. He grabs hold of one hand with the other and it feels no
different than normal. All of those touched begin to speak
about what just happened and asking what this is. As they
speak, people start to respond, "I understand you! You are
speaking my language now!" Every one touched now hears
every other person in the room speaking their native
tongue. Barry can actually hear everyone speaking in
English. Peter stands to quiet the room and after a short
while, he has everyone's attention. He is about to speak,
but is preceded by another voice. This voice is not of
anyone in the room but seems to come from all around.

"I have given you the gift of the Holy Spirit. I have
removed all barriers to you and all things will be clear to
you now. Share the stories of Jesus and prepare yourselves
for a time to come. Many of you will be tested by those
you are sent to, but be true to the teachings and the Spirit
will remain with you always."

The voice then fades away and all is quiet. But those
who had not been touched by the light are now discussing
what is happening. From their comments, Barry concludes
that they did not hear the voice and cannot see the glow
that those who are touched can see. They think the
reactions are those of drunken men. So Peter, who is still
standing, quiets the room once more. "Fellow Jews and all
of you who live in Jerusalem," Peter starts, "let me explain
this to you." For the next several hours, everyone glows as
the stories of Jesus are told back and forth. Barry tells
some of the story. By the time the glow dissipates,
everyone in the room has come to know the same Jesus
that Barry knows and there is now a feeling of anticipation
among them, where only doubt existed before.

After that, each representative goes out to the others of their group who are waiting for news of what is happening. All of the groups gather with the disciples and about three thousand were baptized that day. Most of the groups then pack and begin the journey back to their native lands, taking the story of Jesus with them.

THE ADVENTURE BEGINS

The months following the disciples return from the mountain sees the beginning of the church. Barry preaches alongside the other disciples in the temple courtyards. It is a rough time as many of them are arrested and some of them are beaten. Some of the converts don't last long. They flee at the first sign of troubles, but many more remain and the word is spreading. Shira is not happy with the risks that Barry takes, but she understands that he has been called and cannot turn away now. She does her best to be the dutiful wife and tend to his occasional injuries.

Soon, it is time to depart Jerusalem. A meeting is called among the twelve and plans are made and resources divided. Barry and Shira were going to sell the wagon and Ruffy when they joined the disciples, but the group deems to keep them as they prove very useful at times. And so, Barry takes the wagon along with the biggest contingent of disciples and supplies and heads north. He leaves Jerusalem with one hundred and forty-two disciples. Barry smiles as he is leaving the city walls, leading the donkey and the wagon.

""What are you smiling about?" Shira asks as she walks beside him.

"This is the second time I'm walking north to begin an adventure," muses Barry.

"Second time? I don't understand."

"It's not important."

"What? Stop that… Tell me," begs Shira playfully.

"Well, I told you that I don't really know much of where I come from," Barry says, weighing how much he can really divulge. "But, I remember walking north, starving and lost, when I came upon the caravan that brought me to Timnah… that brought me to you. Now, I'm headed north again, and we shall see who God is leading us to now."

Barry's troupe moves slowly to the north. They are welcomed in most towns where they camp for a few days and share the Gospels that have yet to be written. With each stop, one or two disciples stay behind and a few more head east and west. They stop in one village and Barry is talking, when a small girl is brought out on a litter and laid at Barry's feet. "Master, we have heard the stories of how you have healed the sick. Please heal my daughter." The father has mistaken Barry for Jesus, or maybe Peter, and now he hopes Barry will heal her.

"Me?" Barry thinks. "I've seen Jesus do it… Peter did it… Matthew did it. But, I'm just me… I'm just Barry." He looks around and all eyes are on him. "I'm not Jesus…" Barry says apologetically. What now? What was it that the apostles had to heal? Jesus had told them they possessed all power. Then he sees Shira's face beaming at him and she nods as if to say, "Go ahead - do it!"

"I'm wrong," Barry thinks to himself. "I'm not just Barry any more. I'm the apostle Matthias. I was appointed by Jesus himself. I can do this." Barry bends down and opens his hands towards the girl. He prays silently, "Jesus, my friend, heal this girl through me... hear me. Heal her that they may believe." He lays his hands on the girl's body, but nothing seems to be happening. He continues to pray. Then, his hands start to grow warm. This is followed by a tingling that begins in his arms and pulses up his body. Suddenly he feels as if he's wrestling with something he can't see. His arms lock up and the tingling becomes a burning sensation, like his muscles are straining, but there is nothing he can see that's causing the resistance. Just as the burning starts down his back and his arms feel like they are about to cramp, everything stops. He jerks his hands off the girl and begins to rub his hands gently to restore the feeling back into his fingers as he continues to stare at her face. After a few seconds, the girl opens her eyes and sits up on the litter. There is a gasp from those gathered and the father starts to cry. But the biggest gasp is inside Barry. "Papa!" she cries as she hops up and they hug. "Thank you, master," the man says as he picks up his daughter into his arms.

Barry corrects the man about who he is and who Jesus is and then continues to tell them the miraculous stories of Jesus. Later that evening, after he has eaten, Barry excuses himself and walks out into the fields outside the village. He stands bathed in starlight and looks up at the stars as they twinkle and sparkle. He looks down at his own hands and marvels at what he did this day. "I healed a little girl today," he whispers. "How did I do that? I have no idea what that was. Some transfer of energy? Some channel of God's energy?"" He looks skyward and whispers, "You didn't warn me about this part, Jesus. No wonder you were always worn out and tired. You healed many... I only healed one little girl and I thought it was going to kill me!" He turns to walk back to the house where they were staying. "Was that the 'plain, old' Holy Spirit?" he wonders. "Or did I receive a 'super' dose of Holy Spirit that day in the upper room? Or can anybody who believes do this? Maybe if I had believed before I came here like I believe now, maybe I could have healed someone back home. Perhaps it is not me at all, but the people I heal that are different. They come expecting a miracle... hoping beyond expectations that it will happen. And when it does happen, they are grateful. They don't try to analyze it. They don't say, 'That's impossible' and look for gimmicks. They simply accept that it can be done, so it comes to pass. Perhaps we quit seeing great miracles because we quit believing they were possible." Barry heals a small boy about five years old a week later and then an old blind man after that. And every time it happens, he is at a loss for words to try to explain it, so he finally quits trying. Every time he heals, the easier it becomes. It still drains him, but he learns to relax more and he recovers faster.

Almost four months later, Barry and a few dozen disciples arrive in Sinope, their trek north coming to a halt. To the north are miles and miles of Black Sea. After two weeks, most of the disciples that remain head east and west along the coastlines. Some news of Jesus has already spread to this once great port city. When the Greeks ruled the world, many shipping routes came through Sinope on their way to Athens. Now, as goods go to Rome, the shipping routes have shifted south through cites like Ephesus. Barry can see that this is a city trying to recreate itself. There are many unemployed and poor here as the wealth of commerce has declined.

Within a few weeks, Barry establishes a small core group meeting in homes on a regular basis. With each meeting, there are a handful that come and commit their lives to Jesus and some to be healed. But Barry is uncertain just how strong their faith is, as they have yet to be put to any test. Soon, there are only a few houses big enough to accommodate the crowd and, eventually, they have to split up. Meanwhile, the procurator of this province takes very little notice of them. Barry is not sure if it's because he doesn't know of them or doesn't care. Either way, Barry does his best to keep a low profile as rumors are heard from Rome. The emperor Tiberius is taking an unfavorable notice of this new, radical religious group.

The church, as it is, has been going about four months. Barry is able to do some smith work every now and then for money to feed Shira and himself. For the first time since leaving Timnah, they can relax. Their lives are becoming routine and the stress has given way to happiness and leisure. Barry comes home one evening very tired and as he walks through the door, Shira says, "I have something for you to do, Oded." Shira is the only one that still calls Barry by that name, and she only does it in private.

Barry flops down on a chair and asks, "Can it wait?"

"No," Shira says as she puts a lid on her pot, "it needs to be done right away."

"Fine, what is it you need me to do?" Barry sighs.

Shira comes over and sits on his lap. "You need to pick a name for your child," Shira says as she caresses Barry's face with her hands.

"My...child? Really?" Barry chokes out. Shira nods her head and smiles broadly. Barry hugs her and then places his hand on her stomach. "When?" Barry asks wide-eyed.

Shira laughs, "Not for a while." She gets up and goes back to her cooking and humming a soft tune.

Barry sits in disbelief. "When?" Barry laughs in his thoughts. "Like she's going to have a due date to give me. That's funny. All she knows is it will be 'in a while'. No tests, no sonograms, no examination, no birthing classes. It'll just happen 'in a while'."

Before Shira delivers, she wants to go back to Timnah. Not because there is a shortage of capable midwives in Sinope, but because she is homesick and wants to share the event with family. Barry agrees and they make plans to go back to Timnah. This would be the first test for his new church. Would they continue to function without him there? Barry leaves instructions and the two of them head home. Barry puts Shira, who is somewhere in the beginning of her eighth month, into the small wagon and they are on their way.

It is a long way home and Shira does her best to cope, but it is a miserable ride for her most of the time. When Barry and Shira arrive at Timnah, Migda comes running out of the house. "Shira! You're back." Alon hears her and starts out to greet them from the courtyard. When Shira throws back the blanket covering her little surprise, both the women start to shriek and talk really fast and blessing begin to flow like water. Barry helps Shira off the wagon and she and Migda go inside the house. Alon comes out the gate and he and Barry hug.

"How are you?" Alon asks.

"Good," Barry responds.

"And Shira?"

"Well," Barry says very matter-of-factly motioning towards the house, "you can see for yourself."

Alon laughs and slaps Barry on the shoulder.

"Even after I got used to being married, I never pictured myself as a father," Barry continued. "Shira is so happy, but when I think about it, it scares me to death."

"Ah," Alon scoffs and waving his hand, "there's not really that much to it. Besides, it's the woman's job to raise them anyway. All you have to do is teach them... if it's a boy. In that way, I had it easy; I had two girls," Alon says with a laugh.

"Yeah. I hadn't thought about it that way."

Barry was still stuck in his twenty-first century mind, worried that he would be inadequate to the task of helping raise his child. They then talk about Sinope and the work that Barry is doing there. It has been a little more than two years since they left to go chasing Jesus. Barry hears "Oded!" cried out and he turns to see Bracha. She runs up and hugs him. She's grown taller.

"My, my," Barry says, "Someone has taken the Bracha I knew and left this beautiful young woman in her place."

"And the boys are starting to notice that too," Alon chimes in.

"Papa!" Bracha chides visibly embarrassed. "Where is Shira?"

"Shira?... Who?" Barry teases. Bracha gives him a stare. "Inside with your mother, of course" says Barry. "And she has a surprise with her."

"A surprise?" Bracha asks excitedly as she runs off to the house. After a few seconds, Barry can hear the next round of shrieks from inside. Barry just shakes his head while Alon laughs.

BACK ON THE ROAD

Not much is changed. Alon and Migda look the same. Ditza is moving slower, but still gets around pretty well. Bracha is the only one that surprises Barry. She's filled out into a beautiful and graceful young woman. Many afternoons, Barry comes out of the house to see her talking with a boy over the fence around the courtyard. Barry also takes every one of those opportunities to tease her about it too. It is a little more than a month before a new baby boy enters into the world. Even though Barry is still 'Oded' to the family, Shira names the child Oded since Barry's name is now Matthias and Oded is no longer his 'official' name. Barry is still in shock that he's a father and has no opinion on the name. Both mom and son come through the ordeal just fine. Shortly thereafter, there is a trail of women like ants coming and going to see the baby and offering blessings. Between Ditza, Migda, Shira and Bracha, Barry doesn't get to spend much time with his son. He does enjoy more than one drink at the tavern in honor of his new son, however. At the appointed time, they take Oded to be consecrated and circumcised. Barry uses this time to preach in the town square. Many come to listen and only some remember him as Alon's apprentice and are amazed. Even fewer seem to remember him as the beggar that sat in front of the synagogue, as they paid him little attention then, other than to toss a coin his direction. But Barry recognizes all the faces of those who used to throw him coins as a beggar. And now they sit and listen to his stories and they ask questions about this man, Jesus, and some believe.

But now it's time for Barry to return to Sinope. The good-byes are difficult for Shira. She hugs everybody for a long time before Barry helps her into the small wagon. Migda hands her the baby and hugs her as best she can one last time.

"God's blessings," Alon says.

"We'll be back again. I promise," Barry says as he climbs onto the wagon.

"Keep the baby warm," Migda admonishes.

"I will, mama," Shira replies.

"Good fortune," Bracha wishes them.

The wagon slowly pulls away. Shira turns and waves to everyone and they wave back. Once again the wagon turns the corner and her family and her home disappear. She turns back around and looks at Barry with her large brown eyes. "We'll be back," Barry says again. "I promised! I can't break my promise, now can I?"

"No," Shira says as a smile creeps onto her face, "you cannot do that." She rests her head against Barry's shoulder as she wraps Oded in her arms. "It was good to be home... if it was only for a while. Thank you." Barry kisses her on the forehead and they start their journey back.

Barry has no idea what he will find when he gets back. After a few weeks, Barry arrives with his new addition in Sinope. He is pleasantly surprised upon meeting with the leaders that the church body has actually grown in his absence. It gives him hope that the church is sustainable here. However, they also report that the procurator there has been asking questions about the group.

"We have added thirty-five to our numbers in your absence," says one leader.

"That is wonderful," Barry replies.

"Most of them are farmers that live past the east side of the gates," reports one.

"Oh, but there is also that miller's family that talked to you at the market. Right before you left," adds another.

"Oh, Yes. I remember them. Did his brother come too?" Barry responds.

"No, not yet. We've also gotten word that Icesias has started asking about us," reports another.

"Icesias?" Barry muses, "I wonder what he wants. Has anybody been arrested or detained?"

"No. He has not been seen outside the palace for a month."

"Be of good courage," says Barry. "Jesus stands for us. Do not live in fear."

Barry decides to try and keep as low a profile as possible; just in case there are problems. Another two weeks passes and there comes a knock on Barry's door at supper time. Barry walks to the door as Shira sits with Oded and Barry can see the look of worry on her face. He opens the door and two soldiers stand outside.

"Are you Matthias, priest of the Jewish king god?" asks one of the soldiers.

"I am Matthias," Barry responds, "and I am a disciple of the Jewish god."

"Governor Icesias has requested your presence immediately."

"Immediately," Barry says very matter-of-factly to Shira as she comes to him.

"I don't like this," Shira says softly. "Something bad is about to happen."

"Don't worry. Watch over Oded and I'll be back. I promise," Barry says and he kisses his son on the head as he looks up from Shira's arms.

Barry follows the two soldiers as they walk him back towards the center of town. It's winter now, and though it doesn't get very cold, the sun is already gone and the night has a crisp feel to it. They come to what looks more like a library than a palace or a government building. Much of the town is in ruin and decay now that the big money has gone elsewhere. The old Greek buildings that remain are being torn down to make room for new Roman ones. Once inside, they lead Barry to a room and tell him to wait. The room is scantly furnished as there is very little art or decor. The days have long passed that items of luxury come through this town.

Barry stands towards the center of the room. The eerie quiet makes even his breathing echo from the walls and the dim lamps cast the corners of the room into a rich darkness. Soon, a very drawn man enters the room followed by the two soldiers that brought Barry. He gives Barry a studious stare, but says nothing, as he walks past and in behind Barry. "So," he begins in a very exhausted tone, "You are a priest of this Hebrew god?"

"I am a disciple and a teacher of his word." Barry replies without making eye contact.

"And this god, does he do as you ask?" the man asks as he walks back in front of Barry.

"He does what he wants. Sometimes, I ask things of him. If he wishes, he will grant them."

The man sits in one of the chairs next to a table with a thud, as if all his strength is gone. "My name is Icesias. I am governor over this forsaken spit hole and all that surrounds it. It is not enough that Rome has graced me with this position, but now my only son is dying. I want you to call on your God to heal my son."

Barry can see that Icesias is desperate and that this situation has taken a toll on him. "I can try," says Barry.

"Try?" Icesias declares. "I have heard stories about how you have healed people all around this city. Do you deny this?"

"My God has healed many through me. I have not the power myself."

"But your god has healed many, yes?"

"He heals those who have faith in him, yes. Will you commit yourself to him in faith and repent of your sins?"

"I am a Roman prefect! I have no sin! And I hold neither allegiance nor contempt for your god. I simply want my boy healed." He turns to the soldiers very agitated and commands, "Take him!"

The soldiers take Barry to another room, closely followed by Icesias. In a room barely lit lays a small boy about twelve years old. He is in a coma and has a very high fever. His breathing is shallow and he's turning an ashen white color. "Heal him! Heal him now!" demands Icesias. Barry moves to the side of the bed and gently places his hands on the boy. Verbally, he begins to pray for the boy, but inwardly, he asks God's protection for himself and his family. As much as Barry wishes that God will look favorably upon this situation, the boy is not healed. Barry doesn't know if it because of God's will or his own weakness and concern for himself that prevents it. Finally, Barry turns and says, "I cannot heal your son."

Icesias becomes enraged. "Seize him!" he snaps to the soldiers. "Put him in prison until his god changes his mind!"

As Barry is being led away, he thinks to himself, "I *hate* it when Shira is right."

Barry sits on his small stone bench and stares at the stars through the small barred window towards the top of his cell. Both hands and both feet are chained to the wall with heavy shackles that Barry has tested repeatedly hoping for a flaw in their durability. The air hangs heavy and all is silent. It is the eighth night he has sat here praying to God to release him. No one has been allowed to see him and he misses Shira and Oded. This is the first time they have been forced apart. He can see her smile in his dreams and can smell her hair and feel her gentle touch. His eye lids grow heavy and he nods off to sleep.

In his mind, Barry hears a clinking sound that seems to be out of place. He plays the game where he tries to guess what made that noise without actually opening his eyes and waking up all the way. Then he hears the noise of a cell door unlocking. To hear that at this time of night was very unusual. So, Barry pries his eyes open and tries to see what is happening as he blinks and waits for his eyes to adjust. He raises his hand to wipe his eyes and realizes that the shackle has come off. This snaps Barry awake and he looks around the cell. All his shackles have come off and the cell door is cracked open. "It's about time," Barry whispers. "Sorry! I mean, thank you!" he adds. He gets to his feet and stretches a little. He peers out into the corridor and there are no guards. Barry quietly swings the door open and makes his way down the corridor to the stairs leading out into a courtyard. Once again, a careful check reveals no guards. Barry steps out into the courtyard and sees that the gate to the road is also open. He walks as quickly and as quietly as his feet will take him to the gate. Once outside the gate, he sees a figure approaching in the shadows and Barry's heart races.

"Dear God," Barry begins to pray, "I have never killed a man before. But if this is a guard..."

"Matthias!" comes a loud whisper out of the shadows.

"Who is that?" asks Barry. The figure approaches closer. "Andrew!" Barry quietly exclaims. "What is going on?"

"Let us talk of that away from here," the Apostle Andrew says as he tugs on Barry.

"Great idea," Barry replies as they begin to quickly walk away. Once they are at a safer distance, Barry once again asks, "So, what is happening?"

"We have to get you out of here. Icesias' son has died. I was passing this way and the church here in Sinope got word to me that you had been imprisoned. I prayed to God for you to be released."

"That's interesting," muses Barry, "I prayed for the same thing. Why did you have to come, I wonder?"

"Only God knows. But you are free now and we must get you out of the city."

"I will pack up my stuff immediately."

"It's already taken care of," Andrew assures him. It is then that he sees his little wagon in the road. It is packed and there is a group of people waiting for him. Barry approaches and Shira comes out of the crowd to embrace him. A wave of comfort and relief rushes over Barry now that she is back in his arms. Andrew separates them and says, "You must go now!"

Barry takes Shira and helps her into the wagon. One of the women hands Oded to her. "Where should we go?" Barry asks Andrew.

"Go to Sebastea. It is outside of Icesias' control and it is large enough you can lose yourself there. You can get there in three days if you hurry and don't stop to camp. I will stay here and look after the flock for a short time. Icesias does not know me. We will cover your escape."

"Go with God, Andrew. And thanks."

"You too. Peace be on you, Shira."

"Thank you, Andrew," Shira says as she waves.

Barry urges the donkey forward and they disappear into the night. Andrew is partly correct. Icesias does not know Andrew, but he is successful in getting some in the church to tell him how Barry escaped and who Andrew is. He brings Andrew into the center of town and has him stoned. Out of fear, no one from the church helps Andrew and he is left for dead. That night, Jesus appears to Andrew and heals him. Before leaving, Andrew appears to those of the church and many are strengthened in their faith and vow to dedicate themselves wholly to the Christ. Barry learns of the story several weeks later.

AND SHE MAKES TWO

A little more than two years pass from that dreadful episode in Sinope. After learning of the fate of Andrew, Barry returns to Sinope twice to check up on the church in that span. Barry also establishes a church in Sebastea where the three of them live during this time. This is a large city with many tradesmen and craftsmen and Barry finds work readily. There are poor here also, but fewer here than was in Sinope. Conditions are much better and the government has many more concerns that make the church fall very low on the radar. They enjoy a certain anonymity here that was absent in Sinope. This causes the church to grow rapidly and within the two years many teachers and leaders emerge. Barry is thinking about leaving here and moving on as he comes home on this evening.

"Shira," Barry says as he enters the house, "I've been thinking about the church here..."

"You are always thinking about the church here," Shira interrupts sarcastically.

"Papa!" Oded yells as he runs, interrupting Barry's thoughts.

143

"Hey, little man," Barry tells Oded as he picks him up. "Did you help mama today?"

"Oh, he was a big help when he ripped the sewing I was doing and dumped the clean clothes on the floor." Shira says as she pokes Oded with her finger.

"Yes, well... I think the church is strong enough to stand on its own now. I'm thinking about leaving," Barry says returning to his thoughts while playing with Oded.

"Can we go back to Timnah?" Shira asks in anticipation.

"Sure, why not. I guess we could take a break and go home," Barry muses.

Shira hugs him and says, "That is wonderful news." Barry puts Oded on the floor and sits down. "Speaking of wonderful news," Shira continues casually, "I was hoping we could go home because... I'm with child again."

"What?" Barry exclaims. He jumps up and picks Oded up and spins him around and says, "You're going to have a little brother..."

"Or a little sister," Shira interrupts.

"Yeah. It doesn't matter. We are going home!" Barry turns Oded upside down and Oded giggles.

Barry and Shira return to Timnah, as Barry had promised, with a bigger surprise than they anticipated. Bracha is also with child and is due within weeks. Bracha married a boy named Zachariah, a shepherd's son who stands about the same height as Barry and has a very plain look about him. Although he always smells of sheep, he is a pleasant fellow and Barry and Shira warm up to him quickly. Barry spends some of his time helping Alon and some of his time speaking in the town. He begins a small fellowship, including Alon and Zachariah, which meets regularly. Now with several months to work with, Barry begins a small church there. Since they are a casual three day journey from Jerusalem, Barry periodically goes and spends three to four days catching up on the news and what is happening.

Shortly after Barry and Shira arrive, Bracha gives birth to a girl and names her Mary, after Zachariah's grandmother. Shira goes over to Bracha's home quite often to help her sister with the baby. Though she never tells Barry, Shira has been praying for a girl as well. Just as the summer starts, Shira gives birth to Ditza, a bouncing baby girl. This makes great, grandmother Ditza pleased beyond measure to have a girl named after her. Barry is just returning from Jerusalem when she is born and, this time, he makes sure he gets his baby time. Barry didn't think he could love anyone as much as Shira, but from the day she was born, Ditza put her clamp around Barry's heart and he is hooked for life.

Barry is standing by the gate to the courtyard at mid-morning, staring out to the horizon as the sun climbs the sky. Shira walks by with Ditza and says, "I'm going to Bracha's for a while. And then, I'm going to stop by the market for mama and then I'll be home."

"Where is Oded?" Barry asks.

"He wanted to stay with mama. She's watching him." She pecks Barry on the cheek and Barry opens the gate. "Are you alright?" she asks. Barry nods. "Bye."

"Love you," Barry says.

"You too," Shira responds.

Barry resumes staring. "I am so far from where I thought I would be," he thinks to himself. "I was so sure that money and fame would make me happy. Now, here I am... No real money, no real property and nobody waiting for me to come out of some meeting so I can make some decision that will drive some company up the charts. No one waiting for me to arrive so I can sign a book that will gather dust on a shelf for years until they sell it back or give it away. No one pestering me to write a best-selling sequel.

I have nothing that I wanted. But, I got everything I ever needed. I have a family to love and who loves me. I'm serving God like no one in my own time could imagine. I know that it will eventually cost me my life, but I don't care. I fear not for myself anymore, but for my family. I can't bear the thought of leaving Shira to fend on her own someday. I must trust that God has it all under control. 'Put your life into faith, Matthias. Faith that I know what I'm doing' Jesus told me." Barry looks upward and says, "I am!" He turns and walks back into the house.

Barry leaves to go to Jerusalem once more. This time it is to figure out where to go next. When he arrives, he is walking down the street and passes a familiar face as the man walks with purpose and with his head down. "Who would say that Geber was ever so busy as to pass up an old friend?"

Upon hearing his name, he looks up and spots Barry. "Matthias!" he exclaims and then covers his mouth with his hand. He looks around to see who has heard him and then pulls Barry over to a wall.

"What's wrong, Geber?" Barry asks in a hushed tone.

"I didn't mean to speak so loud," Geber explains. "I was just so happy to see you."

"And that's a bad thing?"

"No, it's just things have changed. Have you not heard?"

"No," Barry says in bewilderment, "I have just arrived from Timnah."

"Tiberius is dead. It happened about eight weeks ago and word is just beginning to reach us. Caligula is now emperor. The persecutions of those who follow our Master have greatly increased around Rome and are spreading. Come; let us get out of the street. I was just on my way to meet Matthew." Geber grabs Barry by the arm and tugs at him to come.

Geber leads Barry to a house and knocks at the door. A man opens the door and lets them enter. Once inside, Barry sees three men sitting and talking. One is Matthew, the second is James, the brother of Jesus and the third is someone Barry has never seen. "Hey," Geber announces, "look at what stray followed me from town!"

"Mathias," cries Matthew. The three men stand and Matthew meets Barry with a hug. "How are you?"

"I am good." Matthew turns and leads Barry to the others. "James," Barry says as he hugs James.

"It's good to see you again, my brother," James replies.

"And this," Matthew says, motioning to the third man, "is Paul of Tarsus."

Barry's mouth drops open a little and a star struck look crosses his face. "It's so good to meet you at last," Barry says.

"At last?" Paul asks.

"Oh, ah... never mind."

"Sit," says Matthew and they all sit.

"I hear you have a son," says James.

"And a daughter now... just born."

"Congratulations," says Matthew. "Mine are so big now; I can't keep up with them. I spoke with Andrew some time ago. He told me what happened at Sinope."

"I was so angry at first," says Barry, "but then I realized... If God had released me when I asked and I had left, it would have been the church that suffered. It could have been destroyed there. But Andrew took the wrath instead. And because of what Jesus did, now they have a strong faith."

"I was there three months ago," Matthew explains. "They have many poor. The church has grown huge."

Then Paul begins to tell Barry some of his stories, beginning with his conversion on the road to Damascus.

Barry listens as if he has never heard any of this before. But this time, he is getting the detail that was never in the Bible. So in some ways, it actually is like hearing it for the first time. They speak into the day about the church and the direction things are going. It's late and now Barry excuses himself so he can get back to his host's house. As Barry says his good-byes, Matthew asks, "May I walk with you?"

"Of course," says Barry. They leave and are walking along the road.

"I fear for our safety with Caligula now in power," says Matthew. "Including you, there are only four of the twelve that are here in Jerusalem. I think we four should leave for a while. I think that would take some pressure off us and off the church here."

"That's not a bad idea, but where? That's what I've been trying to figure out. And God has given me no clues."

"Meet me at the temple courtyard tomorrow. I think I have your answer."

"Hmmm..." Barry hums quizzically. "What are you up to? And should I be afraid?" Barry laughs.

"No. It will be a good surprise. Tomorrow?"

"Tomorrow."

"Good. Blessing on you until then," says Matthew as he turns to walk away.

"And you. Goodnight." says Barry.

The next morning, Barry makes his way to the temple. He finds Matthew standing next to a foreign looking person he does not know. He wanders over as the two men are talking.

"Matthias," says Matthew, "This is Rafa. Rafa, this is Matthias."

"I have already heard so many good things about you, Matthias," says Rafa.

"And they're all true!" Barry says with a laugh. It causes Rafa to laugh as well. "But I'm afraid that leaves me at a disadvantage…"

"Rafa met Phillip on a recent trip..." Matthew started.

"Ah, the man from Ethiopia? The one Phillip baptized?" Barry blurts out.

Matthew and Rafa stare. "How did you know that?" Matthew finally asks.

"Oh, well... I'm sure... ah... someone told me." Barry stammers.

"Yes… well," Matthew continues, "Rafa is headed back home and would like one of us to go with him and bring the stories of Jesus to his people."

"You want me to go to Ethiopia?" asks Barry.

"With Caligula as emperor, we are all in danger. Rafa's people know nothing of Jesus yet. You seem to have a clearer vision than most of us and Ethiopia will put you the farthest from Rome." Matthew explains.

"Well, when you put it that way... I guess we're headed to Ethiopia."

"Wonderful," says Rafa. "I'm so excited."

"Yeah, it's too bad my wife won't be." Barry laments.

Matthew laughs and pats Barry on the back, "God will protect you."

"I'm not sure if that will be enough," Barry laughs.

After agreeing to a meeting place, Barry returns to his host and makes plans to return to Timnah.

THE LAND OF ALMOND EYES

"Where?" Shira asks in disbelief.

"They want me to go to Ethiopia," explains Barry. "We are meeting up with a man named Rafa just south of Jerusalem and then we travel to Ethiopia."

"How far away is it?" she asks dejectedly.

"It's... Well, it's very far. I don't know, exactly."

"Will we ever be back?"

"Eventually..." Barry says in a sheepish voice.

"Eventually? You mean you don't know if we'll be back."

"Yes. We will come back. It just may not be as often as in the past. The kids will love it." Barry says with a strained smile. Shira gives him a sarcastic stare.

Once again, tearful good-byes are said with a promise to return and now the four of them leave Timnah behind and are off to meet with Rafa. They find Rafa's camp at a fork in the road, south of Jerusalem, right where he said he would be. Rafa is the eunuch who met Phillip, gave his life to Jesus and was baptized. He is also a high official in the court of Candace, queen of the Ethiopians. Barry expects to find a tent or two, but instead finds a large camp with many animals and people.

"Wow," Barry exclaims in greeting Rafa. "Do you always travel with a small city?"

Rafa laughs. "This is my queens' caravan. We are bringing many, many things back to my home."

"Ah, I see," Barry responds.

Rafa summons several men. "We leave tomorrow morning," he says to several as they scurry away. To the last he says, "These are the guests I was expecting. Show them where they will stay the night." The man leads Shira and Barry to a large tent with lots of pads and pillows for sitting and sleeping.

The next morning, there is a great flurry of activity as the camp is packed up and animals and carts are organized. There is a man that leads Barry's donkey so he and Rafa can talk as Rafa rides next to them. Barry tries to find out more about where they are going and what to expect, but Rafa is intent of hearing more stories about Jesus. Barry is still apprehensive about this trip. He never traveled outside the United States, except for his fated trip to France that brought him here. When he thinks of ancient Africa, the National Geographic Channel appears and he pictures in his mind half-naked people running around spears and dry, burning desserts or thick, mosquito-infested jungles. He also tried to explain to Shira how their Jewish traditions might have to "bend" a little. This was the biggest adventure either of them had been on and neither of them knew what to expect.

As they cross the Sinai and enter the outer regions of Egypt, it does become hot and dry. It was starting out as Barry's worst nightmare come true. It also brings back memories of his two companions that he buried among the dunes. Many of the lighter-skinned people carry umbrella-like shade to protect them from the heat. Shira is miserable, but Ditza seems unaffected and Oded is too curious and busy seeing everything to let it slow him down. Rafa points out new animals to him as they pass and would pick local fruits and peal them for him to eat or suck on. Barry grew up in the Houston area, so the dry humidity is actually a welcome to him. Two weeks after passing through Egypt, they started to enter the highlands of Ethiopia. Shira is as amazed at the landscape as Oded is. Along the way, they see lots of wildlife. Barry has seen most of them in zoos, but Shira is seeing all of this for the first time. Each night, she can't stop talking about all that she has seen that day. It amuses Barry to hear her so excited, like a small child, and it sometimes surprises him how she views things that he takes for granted. As they ascend in elevation, Barry is pleasantly pleased that the temperature gets quite comfortable.

After a long journey, they get to know Rafa, and Rafa hears many stories of Jesus. Barry also hears many stories of Rafa's home. Rafa doesn't speak much of physical aspects of his home, but instead he mostly speaks of the people's spirit and generosity and compassion. And Barry sees it on display in the villages where they stop. But now they travel near to the capital. "Tomorrow, we shall arrive at the palace of Queen Candace," Rafa says as they travel along. "I have sent messengers ahead so that all will be prepared for our arrival."

"How long has Candace been queen?" Barry asks out of curiosity and just making conversation.

"Oh, Candace is not her name," explains Rafa. "Well, it is her name, but not the name she had before becoming queen. 'Candace' is really more of a title. The queen usually assumes the name of the successor when she becomes queen. The current queen is the actually the third Candace to rule."

"What is she like?" asks Barry. "I've never met a queen before. Is there some custom we need to do? Some special thing we are supposed to say?"

Rafa laughs. "Do not worry, my friend. Queen Candace is a wise and gracious woman. She will not expect you to know our customs. You are coming as my guests. Just be yourselves."

Early in the afternoon on the following day, they arrive at the palace. It is a large sprawling structure of wood and stone. Barry sees that Shira's mouth hangs open as she stares in wonder. It is quite impressive even by Barry's standards. Rafa begins to organize the efforts as soon as he arrives. He speaks to the locals in a broken Greek combined with some sort of local dialect. It is hard for Barry to understand it completely. Barry and Shira are ushered to a room as soon as they arrive. It is a large 'L-shaped' room about the same size of the whole upper floor of the home in Timnah.

Shira gasps, "This is our room? Just the four of us?"

"I guess so," Barry responds, "at least for now."

Shira moves slowly into the room, trying to take in all the colors and textures. The walls are painted with pictures of families and people meeting together. They are very colorful and all the people have large almond shaped eyes. She comes from a very bland world and has never experienced this much stimulation of all her senses. It becomes a little overwhelming and she starts to tear up.

"What's wrong?" Barry asks?

"Nothing... it's all so... beautiful. I'm glad we came," she says. Barry chuckles. She walks over to a large plush bed in the corner. "What is this?" she asks pushing on it with her hand.

"That's the bed."

"It's softer than anything I've ever felt of before. It doesn't feel like straw."

"It's probably feathers."

"Feathers?" Shira quips. "How could anyone find this many feathers?"

Barry laughs. He walks to the partition at the other end of the room. "Hey, come look at this."

Shira peers around the partition. "What is that?"

Barry snickers, "It's a bathtub. You sit in it to take a bath."

"It's so big," Shira says in shock. "Do they fill it with water?"

"Well, yeah. Beats standing in a big bucket. And the water will be warm."

"How do you know all this?" Shira ask suspiciously.

"Oh... ah, Rafa was telling me about it." Barry says sheepishly.

There is a knock at the door. Shira stands at the crook in the room and straightens her clothes like she's expecting someone important. Barry walks to the door and opens it. It is just Rafa. He enters the room followed by three slender, beautiful girls that all look to be about sixteen. They are dressed in long white dresses with decoration of patterns along the bottom. They all stand attentively with hands clasped in front of them.

"Is this room satisfactory?" asks Rafa.

"It's more than anything I expected. It's great!" Barry blurts out and Shira nods her head.

"Who are all these people on the walls?" Shira asks.

"Ah... All these paintings tell of stories and legends of my people. I will tell them to you someday. The ones you see with two eyes are the good guys... the ones you see that show only one eye are evil..." says Rafa with a chuckle.

Then turning to the girls, he says, "May I present to you Abeba, Tenagne and Misrak. They have been made available for you."

"Available?" Barry asks confused.

"Yes," explains Rafa. "They will wait on you while you are here. If you need anything, just ask them and they will provide it for you. They will wash your clothes, watch your children tonight..."

"Tonight?" asks Barry

"Yes. I was hoping you and Shira would join us for dinner. I'll send for you when it's time."

"That would be fine," Barry replies.

"In the meantime, you'll probably want to clean up from the trip. One or all of these ladies will be glad to bathe you if you wish."

"Bathe me?" Barry blurts out in a shocked tone. "Oh... I mean, ah... no. I don't think that'll be necessary." Barry starts to blush at the thought and Shira can do nothing but put her hand to her face in disbelief.

"Do you not have servants in your country?" Rafa asks confused.

"Yes. But we, ourselves, have never had any servants. No," Barry stammers trying to recover from his obvious embarrassment. The three girls giggle but are chided by Rafa.

"Well then, they will be right outside. If you need anything, just let them know."

"Yes. We will," says Barry.

Rafa and the three girls leave the room and shut the door. Shira can't believe what was just said. "They would really stand around and bathe us?" Shira asked as if it were something creepy.

"On second thought," Barry says in a teasing tone, "I am pretty dirty from the trip. Maybe I could use a little help."

"Into your grave…" Shira says sternly with her arms folded. Barry laughs.

Barry and Shira manage to clean themselves and the children by that evening. The girls fetch water for the bath and wash some of their clothes. After they were ready, Shira's curiosity gets the better of her and she invites the girls in to just sit and talk. All three come from small villages in the area, but all of them are fairly conversant in Greek. It is a great honor to the family to have a member serving in the palace. Abeba brings some toys into the room that look like giant wooden jacks and starts playing with Oded. Misrak asks if she can rock Ditza for Shira and sits in chair that pivots similar to an office chair on a pedestal base. Tenagne had disappeared earlier but is now coming in the door to tell them that it is time for them to leave for dinner. Shira is apprehensive about leaving the children, but as they're leaving, it appears doubtful that either child will even know they are gone as the girls have the children's total attention. They kiss the children goodnight and follow Tenagne out the door.

Tenagne leads Barry and Shira down a hallway which opens into a large room where many people are gathered. The room is fifty feet on each side and twenty-five foot tall. In the center of the ceiling is a raised area with small windows which let in air, but are angled and sheltered in such a way as to prevent rain from entering. The four walls are decorated in colorful frescos similar to the ones in Barry's room. They show all sorts of people with those large almond eyes fighting and riding horses and flipped in different positions. They all flow from one to the other interrupted only by archways to hallways leading off in different directions. There are lots of oil lamps that give the room a bright and cheerful glow. The center of the floor is a pit thirty foot square with four steps leading down into it which run the entire perimeter of the pit. In the center of the pit are tables put end to end to form a large 'U'. On the tables is food of every kind of beast and vegetable, and things even Barry has never seen. There are cushions made of colorful fabric next to the tables for people to sit on. People stand on the areas around the pit and by the table in small clusters engaged in conversation. Both Barry and Shira's reaction is one of, "Wow!"

Tenagne walks into the crowd and interrupts a conversation. Barry can then see that it is Rafa who Tenagne alerts to their presence. As Rafa dismisses her and begins to join them, Shira whispers, "I'm scared. What do we do?"

"Relax," whispers Barry. "Just do what they do. If they stand, then stand. If they sit, then sit."

"I don't know …" Shira responds.

"Matthias, Shira. Has everything been satisfactory?" Rafa interrupts as he makes his way to where they stand.

"Wonderful!" exclaim Barry. "We feel like royalty ourselves."

"Excellent!" beams Rafa. "The queen should…" His words are cut short by a cymbal that is struck and a tall, slender woman who appears into the room. Everyone turns and bows. Barry bows and motions to Shira who also bows. The woman then begins to speak with several of the people who are near where she came in. Everyone else resumes their conversations, but now the groups start to mill towards the table. "Come," Rafa says again beaming, "let me introduce you to the Queen Candace."

As they walk towards the table, the queen and those assembled start to take their places at the table. Rafa leads

Barry and Shira to the head of the table to be seated next to the queen. The people gathered are all tall, slender and graceful, standing about a head taller than Barry, even the women. But the queen seems even more graceful and radiates a very regal presence. All of her movements are purposeful. Barry is seated next to her with Rafa on the opposite side and Shira on the opposite side of Barry.

Now Barry has a serious problem. There is roast pork on the table and it smells to Barry like heaven. But Barry is posing as Jewish and there is food that Shira knows is forbidden to eat. Barry silently prays, "Lord, forgive my weakness. But if my mission here is really tied to which foods I eat tonight, then strike me down now... because I really want some of that pork." Barry samples a little bit of everything. God remains silent on the issue, but Shira will be another matter entirely once they have returned to their room.

The night is going well. Introductions are made and it appears that most of the people gathered here are 'public servants' serving the queen in some capacity. Then, Barry and the queen talk in some idle conversation about the trip before she begins to tell Barry of her kingdom. She speaks very good Greek and explains to Barry about the civil wars which have plagued her people until recently. Most of the tribes have been united under one rule, but there is still work to do to gain the trust of the others. She has a brilliant mind and speaks very eloquently. Then the topic turns to why Barry is there.

"So, Rafa tells me of this new God he has come to know." says Candace. "He tells me you are a disciple of this Jewish rabbi."

"He is more than a simple rabbi or a prophet," Barry replies. "He is what the Jews call, 'the Messiah'. He is God's son sent to us on earth."

"Yet he fought no great battles. He did not conquer a nation. He did not drive out the Romans…"

"He fought for the souls of men. Through us he will eventually conquer the world."

"And he accomplished all of this by simply coming here to die?"

"God sacrificed his son to atone for the sin of his people. We have all been redeemed by his sacrifice so that we may all enter his kingdom one day."

"Why would he do this? Is not a son important to the parent? Why not make him a warrior?"

"Would you as queen, sacrifice your child if it were the only way to unite all your tribes in peace that lasted to the end of time?"

Everyone stops eating waiting for the answer as the room draws eerily silent. Candace stares at Barry with a studious expression. After a short time, Candace asks, "And what of loyalty? Does not your God command total loyalty above any other ruler?" Everyone returns to eating.

"Not any other ruler," Barry replies hesitantly. "He commands loyalty that we have no other Gods. His kingdom is not of this world, but of life after death. If a queen stands with God, then their subjects glorify God by serving her."

After a pregnant silence, she sips the last of her drink from her glass and says, "I have enjoyed our conversation, Matthias. We will speak again in the morning." She rises from the table. Everyone rises and bows, including Barry and Shira, and then Candace exits the room. Soon after, everyone else also begins to excuse themselves for the evening and Barry and Shira decide to return to their room.

The next morning, Abeba arrives at the door to tell Barry that the queen wishes to speak with him. She leads him back to the same room where they were the night before, but the tables and cushions have been removed. As soon as Barry enters the room, his nose picks up a strong scent. It is an unmistakable smell that has been repressed into the furthest recesses of Barry's mind. But now, the memory is so strong, it snaps Barry into a trance. He smells... *Coffee*! The aroma winds around his head and beckons him further into the room. He raises his nose and takes a deep inhale. It is just at that moment, one of the servants hand him a cup filled with black coffee. Barry slowly takes a sip and just stands, letting all the pleasure fall from the top of his head down to his toes. "It has been such a long time, my friend," Barry coos in his thoughts.

The queen, waiting for Barry's attention, clears her throat and snaps Barry back into the moment. "I'm sorry," Barry explains, "It been a while since I've had anything as good as this."

Candace smiles and says, "You may teach the ways of your God to any my people who wish to listen, except my warriors."

"As you wish," responds Barry. "May I ask why not them?"

"I'm not convinced of the sovereignty of your God. I need my warrior's allegiance if I am to protect my people."

"I understand." Barry says. He bows and takes his coffee back to the room. "Coffee! One more thing that Shira will not understand," Barry thinks.

THE GOSPEL OF MATTHIAS

Rafa and Barry go to the surrounding villages telling the stories and answering questions. Four weeks pass and Barry has a core group that meet almost daily. Out of the forty or so that are meeting, Barry raises up three men as his first disciples. The first disciple is Azmera. His name means 'harvest'. He is a very friendly sort and very compassionate compared to the others. He sees the big picture and every side of an argument. Tefere, which means 'seed', is the second disciple. He is the serious and studious disciple. He has a question for everything and is very slow to commit to another's opinion. Barry likes Tefere because he keeps Barry 'honest' and the two of them have deep philosophical discussions. Tefere has a little bit more of that Thomas 'show-me' attitude than to Barry's liking, but he's always looking for the deeper meaning that eludes the other two. The last of the three is Fethee, which means 'judgment'. Whoever named him missed by a mile. Judgment is as far removed from Fethee as the east is from the west. He stands out in this land of tall, slender and graceful people as Fethee is rather short and plump. But he has a wonderful sense of humor, a huge heart and is by far the hardest working. He is the first to arrive to the meetings and the last one to leave. Whereas Azmera is Shira's favorite, Fethee is Barry's favorite.

Barry sits down to another supper which Shira hasn't had to cook since they came here and begins to eat. Shira paces and Barry can tell she's upset about something. "What is wrong?" Barry asks.

"You're eating that supper." Shira says very melancholy.

"Yes," Barry responds, "that's because it is supper time and this food is what is for supper. Will you not join me? Do you not like the food?"

"The food is very good," admits Shira.

"Then why won't you sit and have some?"

"I did not cook it. Do you realize that I have not cooked since we got here?"

"Great, isn't it?"

"No. I am your wife. It is my duty to look after you. How can I do my duty if I cannot cook or clean?"

Barry laughs, but Shira doesn't see the humor. "Shira, your duty is to me, isn't it?"

"Yes. Of course."

"Then just love me and raise the kids. Don't worry if you don't get to do everything. The time may come when we leave this place. Enjoy it while it lasts."

"I am not enjoying it. I feel useless. I just flitter all day... like a moth," Shira complains as she sits to eat. "And besides," she adds in a quiet, disgruntled voice, "it's better than I can cook too. Why does it have to taste so good?"

"So funny," Barry thinks, "every woman's dream back home was to never have to cook or clean again. And I have one who complains she can't. Maybe she needs a hobby and should take up painting or write a book..."

Barry snickers to himself. "Maybe I should write a..."
Barry suddenly has an epiphany. "There was no Gospel of
Mathias that was ever found," Barry realizes. "That is it.
That's my contribution. I'm going to write a gospel! It will
be my way of providing the proof I came here for in the
first place. I will write down all of my observations and
then hide the original away to be found later... like the
Dead Sea scrolls." The next day, Barry makes two requests
of Rafa. One is a place to live outside the palace and the
second is some writing supplies. The writing supplies come
almost immediately. Those in the church also start
renovating an old, abandoned dwelling for Barry and Shira
to make their home while they are here.

Several months later, the new house is ready for them to
inhabit. It is a small house, but slightly bigger than the
house in Timnah, which suits Shira just fine. Barry has an
'office' where he keeps his writings. Barry and Rafa now
make plans for a church building as well to serve as a
central meeting place. That summer, the rains come in
monsoon like fashion. It rains all day long for several days
in a row. Barry now knows why they build all of their
structures with high thresholds. Every place had some kind
of flooding, if only three or four inches. The kids love all
the rain as they stomp around in it and play. Shira is not
that appreciative when muddy feet and wet clothes come
into the house. But the rains bring a break from the many
meetings and Barry writes, adding to his volumes and
capturing even the smallest details.

Right after the rains leave, work begins on a new church.
It is a simple square building, one large open room with a
few columns spaced regularly. On three sides, there are
large openings like windows that start almost four feet from
the floor. Later, as the church becomes larger, men and
women will stand on the outside and lean in these

openings. The fourth wall is solid and becomes highly decorated with art depicting all of the stories that Barry tells them. They draw the characters as a way to tell the stories to those who cannot read. Barry is surprised at how many of his flock are literate and can read Greek, at least at a rudimentary level.

Once Barry starts using the new building for meetings, many more come. Many times about two hundred people will cram into the existing floor space to sit and Barry stands in the middle, unable to move but only able to rotate around. About a quarter mile from the church is a crossing where the river grows shallow. Once a month, Barry baptizes the new converts in the river and there is always a line.

Rafa also has Barry preach periodically to the leaders of the different tribes. They come to the palace, and not the church, to hear the stories of Jesus. They come with their servants and all of the trappings of their station in life. Barry tries to stress the austere life that Jesus led, but it never seems to penetrate into their psyche. Barry and Rafa talk after each one of these sessions.

"So, do you think any of them understood the message today?" Barry whines.

"I do not know," Rafa replies. "None of them have expressed interest in being baptized."

"I don't want to say 'I'm wasting my breath on these guys', but ..."

"I know how you feel. But even Jesus did not expect everyone to hear his words, correct?"

"Yes, you are right. And it is not my place to make their decision for them. My job is to tell the story."

Rafa laughs. "And you do a very good job at that!"

Four years have come and gone. Oded and Ditza have grown up in this culture and have learned both Barry's language and the native language. They seem to be quite at home in this environment and they seem to have bonded very well. Oded is now six years old and it is time for Barry to begin teaching him the scriptures and the things all good Jewish boys ought to know. He is very outgoing and shares Barry's curiosity in wanting to know how the world works. Ditza, on the other hand, shares Shira's bashfulness. She will begin to follow Oded on some adventure, but then comes running back home once Oded wanders too far away or something happens to scare her. Ditza is almost an exact duplicate of Shira and follows her around copying her ever gesture. Barry reads to her at night. She has no concept of most of the things Barry reads to her. But, like when Barry and Shira sat on the roof and watched the sunsets when neither of them could communicate, Ditza just appreciates her time with papa and Barry loves the time spent with her.

And so comes the time when Barry and Shira decide to make their first trip back to Timnah for the birth of Barry's third, and last, child. Andrew gives everyone a little bit of a scare as he is born with a breathing problem. But it soon clears up and he seems to be a very healthy and happy boy. Bracha has also had a second child, a son named James.

After returning from their six month sabbatical in Timnah, Barry resumes his duties with the church. They continue to do very well without Barry as Tefere leads worship and Azmera takes charge of reaching new members. Fethee thinks that he may have healed someone, as he prayed over them, but says it might have been a coincidence. Barry is pleased with their progress and speaks to Rafa about possibly leaving. But Rafa has other plans.

Rafa talks Barry into staying and he takes Barry and a large contingent of believers on a missionary trip to the southern regions that are part of Ethiopia at the time. Rafa explains that these tribes are more primitive and can be dangerous, so Barry decides to leave Shira and the children behind. Many of the places they visit are the tribes that have not yet been unified under Queen Candace. Rafa hopes that this new way of living could be the catalyst that helps them all find common ground. With each new region, there are new customs to be observed, new rituals that must be performed in order to gain enough reputation with each group to be able to speak. It is during this trip that Barry does see some half-naked natives running around with spears and rings hanging from body parts and paint on their faces. There are times when the situation becomes dicey, especially as these people speak a very rudimentary local language that Barry doesn't understand at all and Rafa has to translate. But Rafa's reputation and a small, if peaceable, army of disciples helps to keep things under control. Unfortunately, there is not as wide an acceptance of this new Jewish god as there was back in the capital. Certainly, not as many as Rafa had hoped for. It is doubtful that these few converts will be able to hold the course after Barry and Rafa leave. After a long five months and as winter is just beginning, Barry rests his eyes on his familiar home away from home. It was a good trip, but Barry is so ready to be back. The first one to see him is Ditza. "Papa!" she squeals as she comes running from the yard. He grabs her up and holds her in his arms and gives her a big hug.

"I missed you so much," Barry tells her and starts to kiss her on the neck to make her giggle.

"I missed you too," She says after catching her breath from laughing.

"Oded!" Shira says as she runs from the house. She runs to his free arm and hugs him tight. "I give thanks to God that you have returned."

"I missed you too." Barry says as he gives her a kiss.

Ditza pushes them apart and says, "But you missed me more, right?"

Shira laughs. "Of course!" Barry chuckles. Then looking around, Barry asks, "Where is Oded? He must be off in the fields on another adventure."

"No," Shira says with a grin, "he is actually working with some of the craftsmen in town."

"Is he?" Barry asks in a proud tone. Shira nods. "Well, isn't he the big man now? And Andrew? Did he follow Oded to town?"

"No," Shira says, "he's asleep, of course." Then turning to Ditza asks, "Papa is asking silly questions, isn't he?"

"Yeah," Ditza says with a giggle.

The summer comes and goes followed by the next and then the next. And each one brings the heavy rains followed by a mild and pleasant winter. Five years flow by in the beating of a heart. Barry and Shira are surprised that the time has gone by so quickly. Their family and their church are growing and spreading like grape vines racing to find an open space on the trellis. Oded is a young man of eleven now and has some of his father's features. Ditza is beginning to flower at age nine and looks more and more like Shira with every day that passes. Andrew is a handful and wants to be a part of everything as a precocious five year old. Barry stays busy and has written several volumes of paper. It is a beautiful spring day when a knock comes at Barry's door. Barry opens the door and Rafa is standing there with news.

"Good day, Rafa," Barry greets him. "Please, come in."

Rafa doesn't budge. "I have met someone who questions your ability as a teacher," Rafa says in a very serious tone. Barry is confused and stands dumbfounded at Rafa's comment. Suddenly, another figure steps into view at the doorway and says, "I told him you couldn't even teach a Roman to salute."

"Andrew!" Barry exclaims loudly as his hands fly up. Barry reaches to hug him and pulls him into the room.

Shira enters the room saying, "What has Andrew..." But then she sees Andrew standing at the door. "Oh, *that* Andrew!" Shira squeals excitedly as she runs to hug him as well.

"Come in and sit down," Barry commands. The three men sit down in the front room and Shira disappears into the kitchen.

"How are you?" Barry asks.

"I'm good," Andrew responds. "I was at Corinth and needed to leave in a rush."

"Trouble?" asks Barry.

"Let's just say the authorities were asking too many questions to my liking."

Barry and Rafa laugh.

"So," Andrew continues, "the only ship leaving at the time was headed to Egypt. So, I said to myself, while I'm in the area, why not stop in on Matthias and see how he's doing?"

"In the area?" exclaims Barry. "That's not really 'in the area'. What brings you this far?"

Shira reappears with a tray of fruits and bread. "Eat something, Andrew," Shira says. She sets the tray down on a table between the men.

"Thank you," Andrew says to Shira. Turning back to Barry, he says, "We haven't heard from you in a long while. Some people think you're dead. Some have forgotten your name – it's like you don't exist. I was curious how you're doing... if you were still alive."

"Oh, I'm doing well here. I suppose Rafa has told you some of what is happening here."

"Actually, we just met," Rafa says.

Shira returns with cups and a carafe of coffee and places it on the table.

"Oh, Andrew," interrupts Barry, "you have to try this if you haven't already." Barry pours Andrew some coffee. Shira finishes pouring the coffee for Barry and Rafa.

"I was telling people that I came looking for 'The Great Matthias'. One woman in the market directed me to Rafa. He brought me here." Andrew then takes a sip of the coffee and says, "Wow, this is different."

"Good, isn't it?" replies Barry. "So, tell me the news. What is going on out there? I haven't heard anything about what going on."

"The twelve are now traveling again. There is now controversy in Jerusalem."

"Is Caligula still alive?" asks Barry.

Andrew chuckles, "Caligula died two years ago. Claudius is now the emperor. And he has his hands too full with wars in the northern part of the empire to worry too much about us. Times are a little better."

"Two years? I have been isolated here."

"Mama? Papa?" comes a small voice as little Andrew enters the house.

"Come here, son," Barry says softly. He grabs the boy by the shoulders and turns him to face Andrew. "Do you know who this is?" Barry asks his son. The boy shakes his head. "This is Andrew," Barry says.

"I'm Andrew," says the boy as Shira comes back to the room upon hearing her son.

"Yes," answers Barry. "This is Andrew too. You're named after him."

"Me?" Andrew says shocked.

"You saved Matthias' life," says Shira. "Come, Andrew," Shira says waving the boy to her, "you must get washed up so you can help me."

"Bye," says the boy as he runs to Shira.

Andrew looks back to Barry and Barry says, "For what you did at Sinope."

Andrew smiles and says softly, "God did that... but I am honored. Thank you."

After a short silence, Barry stands and says, "So, let me show you around." The three men prepare to leave. "Shira," Barry yells to the other room, "I'm leaving to show Andrew around."

Shira appears in the archway to the room and says in a stern voice, "Don't be late for supper!" Then she says in a more gentle voice, "Andrew, you will eat with us tonight?"

"Of course," Andrew replies. Barry then leads them out the door.

Barry takes Andrew for a tour. After just a short time, Rafa excuses himself and returns to the palace. Barry takes Andrew to the river where the baptisms are done and takes him to meet Azmera, Fethee, and Tefere. Then Barry takes him to the church building.

"This is a church building," Barry says as the two men step into the large room. The sounds of men laboring fill the air.

"It's beautiful," says Andrew. "Very colorful."

"We got too big to meet in homes. This is the first building," explains Barry. "This is where I normally teach. We started out with men wedging in on the floor as I stood right here in the center. Then men started hanging over through the windows there and there," Barry continues, pointing around the room. "But soon, even the windows were full. So then we added another spot," Barry says as he walks through an added archway onto a covered walkway. A short distance away are two more areas also connected to the walkway. One is still under construction as men labor to complete it. Most of them pause momentarily and wave or call to Barry. Barry waves back. "We added this area," Barry explains pointing to the completed addition, "to hold a second group. Tefere, he's the serious disciple you met, he teaches here to new converts as I teach back in the other area to those who have been here a while."

"This is amazing," Andrew says as he rubs his head.

"Now, we are adding this area that they are working on to hold a third group. Azmera will begin to teach new converts and Tefere will take over teaching the more experienced and I will be left to teach those who will be leaders and disciples to carry the teaching away from here. Shira will also use this new area to teach the women."

"Teach women?" asks Andrew slightly puzzled.

"Yes," Barry explains, "I've been teaching Shira. In this culture, women are more equal than in Jerusalem. They even have women warriors here. They are God's creation too. They need to learn a little, at least."

"You have such strange ideas, sometimes," Andrew laments.

"As I recall, the Pharisees said the same thing to the Master on more than one occasion..." Both men laugh.

It is getting late and Barry knows he will hear about it if he makes himself and Andrew late for supper. So they both hurry back to the house and Shira prepares something special in honor of Andrew's coming. After supper is over, Barry shows Andrew his writings. Andrew is confused why Barry would waste so much of his time.

"What is the point?" Andrew asks. "Jesus will return any time now. Who will need to read your writing after that happens?"

"What if by 'soon', Jesus meant compared to eternity? It's been over ten years. What will our children, our children's children use to start new churches if we don't start writing this stuff down. Moses wrote down his inspiration from God. Even God himself wrote down his commandments in stone, if you'll remember." argues Barry.

Andrew laughs, "Yes, but this is different. If he doesn't come in your lifetime, surely he will come in Oded's generation."

"Maybe that's what Isaiah thought too," Barry replies. "Paul used to think so..."

"Yes, Paul always woke up every morning in those early days expecting Jesus to come that afternoon," Andrew chuckles.

"And he may come tomorrow... and he may not. He may come to Oded... and he may not. What if it's hundreds of years until he returns? At least Isaiah's words were written down so that we would have them."

"Alright," Andrew concedes, "point taken. I will speak to the others about your concerns."

PARADISE LOST

Andrew stays with Barry almost a year. He teaches in the church and baptizes with Barry at the river. Barry convinces Andrew that writing down some of the Apostle's thoughts and stories is not such a crazy idea after all. Andrew promises to bring up the subject when he returns to Jerusalem to tell them how Barry is doing. Barry agrees to join him in Jerusalem soon as the twelve are returning to confront many controversies that have arisen between the Christian Jews and the Christian Gentiles. And Barry has the reputation among the apostles for being able to pinpoint, not only the real issue, but also the choices that exist. During the time Andrew is there, Barry is able to prepare Tefere to take his place and has trained up several more disciples to aid in teaching. It is with mixed emotions that Barry and Shira say goodbye to Andrew as he heads back and they make plans to leave.

Barry is in his 'office' spending the whole week trying to sum up the last ten years as they are planning on leaving the next month. He writes directions and reminders for Tefere. Suddenly, he hears the door slam open. Assuming it is one of the kids, he rushes into the front room to see what the emergency is. He is met in the front room by several men from the church who grab and restrain him without a word.

"What is going on?" Barry exclaims. The men holding Barry begin to tie his hands behind his back and bind his feet together. Before Barry can comprehend what is happening, other people are picking up possessions in the room and smashing them to the floor. "Hey! Stop that!" yells Barry. "Somebody tell me what's going on!" he demands, but no words are forthcoming. He then hears Shira struggling in the other room. Another enters the room holding a wiggling and crying Andrew. "Tell me..." Barry begins before he is gagged along with Shira.

"What is happening?" Barry's mind races. "I know these people. They're all from the church. What could drive them to this? Did the queen die? Is this a coup? Why have the church people turned against us? What will happen to us now?" Barry's mind is a whirr as he and Shira are whisked from the room amid continued smashing and breaking of everything in the house. They are being carried away from the house, but not towards the palace.

Shira is still panicking and Barry can hear her crying as they are being carried to the same place. Andrew is not with them. Barry has no idea where Oded and Ditza are now or what is being done to them. Barry is starting to calm down and his mind is starting to try and piece things together. "We're being kidnapped, it appears. If they had wanted to kill us, they would probably have already done it. But why?" Barry thinks. "Nothing unusual happened in the church over the last several weeks. They're moving in a hurry, like they are panicked too. Perhaps they are protecting us from a coup. But why not tell us? Why gag and bind us and carry us off to who knows where?"

The mob carrying Barry and Shira approach the house of someone Barry knows from the church. "They're taking us somewhere familiar, that's encouraging," Barry ponders. "Perhaps they will untie us and explain things now." The mob goes around to the back of the house and opens the door to a storage shed. They shuffle inside and lay Barry and Shira on the ground and then exit quickly. They close the door and Barry can hear them running away. "Or," Barry thinks, "I could be wrong about the untying and explaining part."

All is suddenly quiet with the exception of Shira's whimpers. Barry rolls over and tries to inch closer to Shira until their heads touch. She looks into Barry's eyes with a confused and terrified stare. Barry shakes his head as to try to allay her fears. The sunlight filter's through the cracks between the door slats. The dust dances above their heads for a time stepping in and out of the light. Barry thinks about the children and prays to God for their safety. "What went wrong?" he continually asks himself. "This was paradise. We had everything here, Lord. Was I too comfy? Is that it? Had I become slothful and unmotivated?" Barry thinks.

Perhaps an hour later, the door opens quickly and Oded is deposited next to them and the door is shut again. Oded is not crying and squirms next to Shira and looks over to Barry. Barry shakes his head as if to say, "I have no idea either." The sun is setting quickly as the beams of light fall towards horizontal and then, one by one, fade away. Shira and Oded are drifting in and out of sleep from the ordeal, but they are all stirred when someone can be heard coming. Once again, it is mob sized and Barry prays for their protection. The door swings open and the three of them are lifted up and brought outside the shed. They are stood up in a great circle of people and all is bathed in torchlight.

They are being untied and Fethee step forward from the crowd.

"Are you alright?" asks Fethee in a timid voice.

"No, we're not alright!" Barry says angrily. "Fethee, can you please tell me what is going on here?"

"A Roman garrison came looking for you and your family," explains Fethee.

"Roman soldiers? Here?" exclaims Barry as his anger turns to concern.

"Where are Ditza and Andrew?" pleads Shira.

"The children are fine. They are with Abeba. They were easy to hide. But we had no warning; the soldiers killed some of our people trying to find out where you were. We had to hide you."

Now, it's all starting to come together for Barry. "Which is why... you began destroying the house..." Barry says.

"Yes, we destroyed almost everything in the house. I'm sorry. We told them you offended the queen and that you tried to lead a revolt and we destroyed your house and that we crucified you a year ago."

"Did they buy that?" asked Barry.

"I'm not sure. They seemed skeptical... perhaps the damage to the house looked too recent, but they finally left. Queen Candace was furious. They left after she threatened retaliation for the lives they took."

"Fethee, you didn't destroy the scrolls, did you?" Barry asks nervously.

"No, we did not..." says Fethee

"Good," Barry interrupts. "Everything else can be replaced."

"No," Fethee continues, "when they didn't find you, they burned the house."

"What?" Barry exclaims. "Oh no, no..." Barry takes off running towards the house.

"Matthias wait!" yells Fethee.

Barry runs as he has never run before. He cannot even feel his feet touch the ground. His thoughts are totally consumed on the house. "Please, God, let the writings survive... please..." As he approaches, he can already smell the destruction. He finds the stamina to run all the way there.

But when he reaches the house, Barry is stopped in his tracks. He falls to his knees as his chest heaves and he tries to catch his breath. In the soft moonlight can be seen the house foundation, smoldering and smoking. At the corners of the house, are the remnants of the main posts that still glow with embers. The smell of charred wood sits heavy in the air. Some of the smaller objects have been blown off the foundation and into the yard. Sparks and bits of flame can be seen dancing from time to time across the floor as it finds those scraps left untouched and is fanned by the breeze. "Everything is gone," says Barry to no one in particular. "Everything." It is not until he is snapped out of his trance by a soft pair of hands on his face that Barry realizes that not everything is lost.

"I'm so sorry," Shira whimpers. "I know what those scrolls meant to you."

"No," Barry says with a sigh as he stands up to hug Shira and Oded, "everything that is most important still remains."

They return to the palace that night and Barry has a one-sided conversation with God. "So, that is why there was never a Gospel of Matthias! Or more like an Encyclopedia of Matthias as much as I wrote. Once again Andrew was right. It did turn out to be a waste of time. Well, maybe not a total waste. It did help me, I guess. I just wish I

PROOF!

could have provided a more concrete proof of what happened... A more accurate accounting... But then, where is the faith in that? You had this planned the whole time, didn't you?"

The next morning, Barry returns to the house with Tefere to search the remains by daylight. The light brings no comfort. Barry finds a few unburned scraps, but the story he compiled is gone. The fire did a good job of consuming everything. Barry cannot find anything of value among the rubble and ash. "There is still one thing I don't understand," says Barry. "Why did you feel it necessary to tie us up? Why not just come to us and tell us to hide?"

"Did you not teach us that Jesus gave himself to the Roman authority freely?" asks Tefere.

"Well, yes. He had to in order to fulfill the scriptures."

"We love your family too much to let you do that. So we took you."

"Let me do what?"

"Give yourselves to the soldiers. You have taught us that to die in the name of Jesus is a good thing, right?"

Barry chuckles as he rubs his head and says, "Yes, I suppose I did. But Jesus doesn't expect us to hand ourselves over to our enemies." But then, after a short respite of contemplation, Barry contends, "Well, maybe you've hit on something, Tefere. Maybe if we were truly perfect, that is what we would do. But as we are, dying in the name of Jesus gives him glory... but it not mandatory! Keep yourself alive so you can continue to spread the word."

"I think I understand now," says Tefere. "But tell me, if we had not tied you up and hidden you, would you have stood up to the Romans and died?"

Barry again contemplates the question for a moment or two and finally put's his hand on Tefere's shoulder and says,

"You know, that's a good question. I've never thought about it in those terms before. I've never had to make that choice."

Barry receives word that the queen wishes to speak with him. Barry already knows what she will say. He shows up in that big square room where he stood for the first time some ten years ago, entranced by the smell of fresh coffee. A young man brings him a cup today as he greets the queen.

"You must leave my kingdom as quickly as possible," the queen says in a very matter-of-fact tone.

"I know," Barry says.

"You have been a tremendous influence on my people, but I cannot take on the Roman Empire for the life of a single man. But at the same time, I do not wish to see you leave."

"Ten years ago," Barry says, "I asked if you would sacrifice one of your children to save the kingdom. And so, you do."

"And so, I do." replies the queen slowly. "However, if that were all of it, it would not be so terrible. But now I have puzzle."

"A puzzle?" Barry asks.

"When the Romans came, I thought I would see fear and panic. What I did see was my simple subjects fighting for an idea harder and with more courage than I have seen from many of my warriors. They were willing to sacrifice themselves for you and your God and to stand between you and the Romans with such bravery... I knew then that they were your people, not mine. So I gave them the chance to leave with you, but they refused. They told me they were still loyal to me and would fight the same way to protect their queen. So, before you go, I have one last duty for you to perform."

"Whatever you wish, if it is within my power." Barry answered.

"Baptize me in the name of your God. And Rafa will teach me how to lead with such courage and loyalty."

That afternoon, in the company of about five hundred, Barry baptizes Queen Candace in the same river where hundreds of her subjects had been baptized before her. Rafa is appointed special spiritual advisor to the queen and Tefere is named head of the church. Barry leaves the next day in an empty wagon, filled with only his wife and children, enough food to reach Egypt, and a month's worth of coffee he had talked someone out of. As they pull away, Barry looks at Shira and says, "I think this is the first time we're going home that you haven't been with child."

Shira laughs.

THE CHURCH OF JERUSALEM

Barry and Shira arrive in Timnah just as the month of Hanukkah is beginning. Ditza, Migda's mother, passed away two years earlier. Alon and Migda are looking older to Barry now. It brings to light just how long that they have been in Ethiopia. The town looks and sounds different. Barry meets a young man who is part of the church that Barry started here in Timnah all those years ago. They are still leading groups that are meeting in people's homes, but there are many groups. There is always talk of building a church, but there are some Pharisees in town that stir up trouble whenever it is mentioned. Barry never tells the young man who he is until after he hears the man's stories of Jesus. For the most part, they're still intact, although not as complete in detail as Barry tells them. Barry can already tell there are small erosions in the oral traditions that will eventually be written down; which he had tried to write down.

Since they are so close to Jerusalem, Barry leaves Shira and the children in Timnah once more and goes by himself to see what is happening at the Jerusalem church. After securing a place to stay in Jerusalem, Barry goes to seek out James, brother of Jesus. He finds James with Matthew and Peter.

"Matthias!" exclaims Peter. "It is really you."

"It is really me," Barry responds.

"We heard you were dead," Matthew says. "We received word that the Romans had crucified you in Ethiopia, but Andrew refused to believe that."

"Oh, so they took credit, did they?" asks Barry.

"I don't understand," says Matthew.

"The Romans came looking for me. The Ethiopians told the Romans that they crucified me! They hid me and my family until the Romans left."

"The soldiers probably sent word to Rome that they killed you to save their own hides," Peter says. "That's when we intercepted it."

"Well, they weren't convinced one hundred percent, so I was forced to leave," replies Barry.

"Since you're dead, Rome won't be looking for you here," muses Peter. "Matthew and I were just leaving to go round up more disciples. We are meeting after Hanukkah to discuss issues that have come up. Until then, why don't you stay here and help James get ready?"

"I can do that," replies Barry. "I'm staying with Joab here in town."

"Where is Shira?" asks Matthew.

"She's in Timnah with the kids."

"You had two?" Peter asks.

"Three," Barry says proudly. "Two boys and a girl."

Peter chuckles, "Maybe I should have gone to Ethiopia!" They all laugh.

Two weeks later finds Barry with a house that will hold the family temporarily. It belongs to a friend of a friend who will not be moving into it for several months, so Barry will basically be house-sitting until he can find other arrangements. Barry sends one of the disciples to Timnah to tell Shira of the house and help her pack to come to Jerusalem. Queen Candice did provide them with enough Greek currency to replace most of the necessary items they needed, once they got back to Timnah. Later that week, the disciple returns without Barry's family in tow.

"What is wrong?" Barry asks.

"I do not know," replies the disciple. "Your wife just told me that you have to come to Timnah. She made it clear you must return quickly. I came back as quickly as I could to tell you."

Barry's mind races through all of the possible things that could be wrong. "Is someone sick? Is someone dying?" Barry asks desperately.

"I do not think anyone was dying. But Shira told me nothing beyond that."

"Very well. Thank you for your service. Help me pack and I will leave before sunset," implores Barry.

Barry arrives in Timnah. As he approaches the house, all seems normal. Shira comes traipsing from the house like a little school girl. She has a smile on her face which instantly defuses all of the horrific visions that Barry has been imagining. As Barry enters the courtyard, he also sees Oded working alongside Alon and his son waves at him with only a look of acknowledgement. Alon waves also and the two return to their work. Shira greets him and Barry says, "So what is wrong that I had to come here right away?"

"Who said anything was wrong?" Shira asks quizzically. She grabs hold of his hands and pulls him towards the house.

"Well, I was told nothing except that I had to return immediately. So I assumed that someone was dying." Barry says as he follows Shira up the stairs to the roof. They sit down on the old, familiar bench.

"The shadchan has found a wife for your son," Shira says beamingly.

"Oded?" Barry says shocked.

"No, Andrew... Of course, Oded!" Shira says sarcastically. "I think it is a good match."

Barry is totally stunned. "My Oded? Married?" Barry thinks. "Well, he is thirteen. And that is the age of manhood here. How did this sneak up on me? I never thought of him as being old enough for marriage. Stuck back in my twenty-first century mind, I guess."

"Did you hear me?" Shira asks shaking his arm. "I think it's a good match."

Barry snaps out of his fog. "What does Oded think? Does he love her?" Barry asks.

"He's not completely sure. But, who is ever completely sure? He'll learn to love her like you learned to love me." Shira argues.

"What's her name?"

"Rachel. And she is beautiful. They will make beautiful children."

"I don't have much for a bride price."

"Papa has already said he will give Oded the money. Oded wants to stay here and work with papa and he will pay it off."

Barry, feeling very railroaded, scratches his head and says, "Sounds like a match. So, why did I have to come back here? It sounds like all the decisions have already been made."

"I cannot go talk to her father," Shira says exasperated. "You have to go talk to him and make the deal. You can go right after supper."

"Alright," Barry sighs.

Shira kisses him and says with a beaming face, "I'll send Oded up here." She disappears down the stairs. After a short while, Barry's son comes up the stairs with a lost look on his face. Barry has had that look many times. It is a look that grips the males of the species when they have been out paced, out maneuvered and out witted by the females of the species into doing their bidding. It is a look of no longer feeling in control and not knowing what the future will bring. Oded wanders over and sits down on the bench next to Barry.

"So...," Barry says, not really knowing where to begin, "The matchmaker has found you a wife..."

"I guess so," Oded says very melancholy.

"Have you talked to her?" Barry tries to ask sympathetically.

"Yeah, we talked a couple of times."

"What do you think of her?"

"She's really nice. We talked about a lot of things."

"Do you like her?"

"Yes. I think I do, anyway," Oded says hesitantly. And after some weighty consideration says, "Yes, I do like her."

"Such an honest boy," Barry thinks. "That' how I started out with Shira."

"She's pretty," Oded continues, "and I like being with her."

"How does she feel about you?" Barry asks.

"About the same, I guess. She thinks I'm really smart because I can speak Ethiopian," Oded says with a smirk.

"Well, at least they like each other," Barry thinks. "So, now it is time for the bomb." Barry asks, "Do you love her?"

"I don't know," Oded replies in a panicked tone as he looks at Barry. "When I'm with her, my stomach starts to hurt a little. I feel really good but kind of weak and a little scared all at the same time. But then, after she leaves, I start to feel normal. But then, even thinking about her, I start feeling the same way. I don't know how I'm supposed to feel."

"Poor boy," Barry thinks with smile, "he has no idea how badly he's hooked. He's just a large mouth bass, fighting the line but waiting to be reeled in." Barry pats his son on the shoulder and says, "It was the same way with me."

"It was?" Oded says with giant sigh of relief. Barry could see a large weight lifted from him.

"Oh, yes," Barry continues. "Just the thought of marriage made my palms sweat."

"Mine too," Oded says with a half smile. He begins to think that this is not the end of the world after all.

"And then, when we first got married, I thought to myself, 'Do I love her? Will this work out?' But as we were together, I loved your mother more and more. Now, I can't think of my life without her."

"But how do I know it will be the same with me?" Oded asks.

"You can't. But, from what you've told me, I don't think it can be any other way."

They both smile and Oded is feeling better about the whole situation. But then he gets a serious look on his face and says, "I do have another question..."

Barry sees his son's profound look and says, "Ask me anything. I'll answer it if I can."

"Well," Oded continues, "I do have a few questions about..." he hesitates and then says in a sheepish voice, "you know... *after* we're married..."

"Oh! Of course..." Barry says realizing that he and Oded had never had 'the talk' about men and women.

Shira calls up to them that supper is ready. They both come down the stairs, having completed their manly discussions of all matters related to women, and join the family to eat. The mood is festive and Oded is suddenly all grown up in Barry's eyes. He is amazed at how his perspective changed in only one short afternoon. But Barry is confident that Oded is mature enough and up to the responsibility after their talk. That evening, Barry goes to speak to Rachel's father. Rachel is everything Shira described. She is pretty, polite and very sweet and the deal is made.

Barry travels back to Jerusalem while Shira is busy with the wedding preparations. The day of the wedding arrives, just a month after Hanukkah is over. Barry sees Oded standing under the tent and he is reminded of his own wedding. Life was such a blur for Barry as he remembers all the anticipation of finding Jesus. Wondering how he would juggle his new quest and a new wife. Both the kids are nervous and it shows, despite their best efforts to hide it. Barry thinks about all of the simple pleasures that await his son in this new phase of his life; love, a wife, children. Barry believes that it will be much easier for Oded here; a stable life will help him find his way. Barry sometimes wishes his own life could be more like Oded's. But Barry knows he can never go back now. His life is inescapably woven into God's plans.

Barry comes to Timnah for Hanukkah and stays through the wedding celebration. The wedding goes well. Barry then packs up his wife and their two other children and begins to make the trek to Jerusalem. The good-byes are still as intense, even though they will only be a couple of days away. Shira was so excited during the celebration, but now she has to let her son go and leave him behind for the first time. It was not so easy for Barry either. For all the proud, chest-thumping gestures Barry put forth, there was still a piece of him that was being left behind. The wagon pulls away and the waving is done and Shira snuggles up to Barry. Barry knows this is not Shira's usual snuggle, but more of her 'I want something' snuggle. After a few obvious attempts to get his attention which he tries to ignore, Barry finally smiles and says, "What?"

"What?" Shira says innocently.

"Don't give me 'what?'. You are up to something."

"Well I was thinking," Shira begins, "when we get to Jerusalem, maybe I should find a shadchan there."

"Oded's already married," Barry says absent-mindedly.

"Not for Oded. For Ditza, silly!"

"What?" Barry exclaims in unbelief looking at Shira.

"Well," Shira says very matter-of-factly, "she's almost twelve years old." Barry exhales a huge sigh. He hangs his head and slowly shakes it back and forth. "What?" asks Shira.

THE CONVERTS

After Barry returns to Jerusalem, the disciples start to gather. It has all the trappings of a grand congressional debate between Republicans and Democrats with people lining up on both sides of the aisle, determined to give neither quarter nor ground. The big issue that is beginning to rub the faithful raw are those pesky Gentiles that hold little concern for Jewish law. The evening prior to the big meeting, Barry meets with Peter, Matthew and Paul to discuss strategy. That evening, Barry gets up to make his way home. Peter asks, "May I walk with you?"

"Of course, my brother," Barry says.

They bid their host and Matthew and Paul a good evening and depart. As they slowly walk, Peter says, "You didn't say much this evening, Matthias."

"There wasn't much to say beyond what was already said," Barry replies.

"I don't know. We are Jews after all. One of the things that make us different from the world is circumcision. Perhaps it isn't as unreasonable as Paul suggests."

"Let me ask you this, my brother. If you were not already circumcised, would you want to endure it now? Would all the pain make a difference in how you view God? Would circumcision done tomorrow make you a better disciple?"

"No. You're right. It would make no difference," admits Peter.

"If pain were the only requirement to enter into God's presence, then surely the poorest Gentiles have suffered as much as the poorest Jews under Rome's boot. Why must we inflict even more pain upon them? We would be arguing the same way were we in their position."

Peter chuckles. "I trust Paul, but sometimes he has such radical ideas..."

Barry stops walking and turns to Peter, "Do the Pharisees not call us 'Radical'? These are radical times, my friend."

"I suppose you are right," Peter muses.

Barry puts his hand on Peter's shoulder, "Trust me, Paul will raise up such a church among the Gentiles... He will be remembered long after you and I have been forgotten."

Peter starts to walk again, "You think so?"

"I do. This will eventually be the church of the Gentiles." Barry proclaims.

"What?" asks Peter shocked. "I can't believe you of all people would say that. The Jews have always been God's chosen."

"Yes, they are," Barry contemplates, "and God will never abandon the Jews. But, we have always been stiff necked. Moses even said so. We take our God for granted because he has always been there for us. We have never known a time without God; even in the exile. It is the Gentiles, who have never known God and who are finding him for the first time... they are the ones on fire in their hearts. They will be the ones to send forth the word like a wildfire spreading out of control. It will be that way... for many generations to come."

"It is not only Paul who has some radical ideas," Peter laughs. "I'll see you in the morning."

"Yes, Goodnight" says Barry as they part company.

The next morning, everyone starts to assemble and the battle lines begin to be drawn in the murmurs and the whispers. The Pharisees among the group try to rally support for their cause. After everyone has settled for the most part, Peter stands to speak. "My brothers, one and all, you have been called and we gather together to settle some of the uncertainty that has entered into the Master's teaching. We need to be of one accord and be consistent in what we stand for. That has been the wishes of our Master who sends us from the beginning. That day, in the upper room, when the spirit came upon us and we were united as one mind."

One of the attending stands and says, "How can we be one? We are Jew and Gentile. How can we be one when some of us do not follow the law of our God?"

As he sits, another blurts out, "We all should be Jews. The gentiles need to be circumcised and follow the laws of Moses."

A cacophony of arguments and viewpoints erupts with each man talking louder than the previous to be heard. Peter tries to regain control, but there is none to be had. After several attempts, Peter begins to quiet the crowd as tempers subside. Finally, Peter says, "Brothers, I have told you that, some time ago, God send me to the Gentiles that they might hear the message of our master, Jesus, and believe. He gave to them the Holy Spirit, just as he did to us, right in front of my eyes. God did not discriminate between us and them, for he purified their hearts by faith. I think it is wrong of us to test God by putting on the necks of Gentiles a yoke that neither we nor our fathers would bear." As he scans the room and points out to the crowd, Peter continues, "How many of you here, if you were not circumcised already, would be ready to have it done to you now?" A deathly hush falls upon the room. Most everyone assembled knows someone who has undergone the procedure as an adult and knows of the pain and agony that accompanies it. "We believe," Peter says, "that it is through the grace of our Master, Jesus, that we are saved... just as they are."

Peter then yields the floor to Barnabas and Paul. They begin to tell wonderful stories about the signs and wonders that God did among the Gentiles through them. When Paul and Barnabas are finished, James stands up to speak. "Brothers," he says, "listen to me. God has given us clear sight to see that God cares more about our hearts. It is written: 'After this I will return and rebuild David's fallen tent. Its ruins I will rebuild, and I will restore it, that the rest of mankind may seek the Lord, even all the Gentiles who bear my name, says the Lord, who does these things.' It is my judgment, therefore, that we should not make it difficult for the Gentiles who are turning to God."

From the back comes a voice, "Well, perhaps they do not need to be circumcised, but what of the law? Surely they could honor the law of Moses."

"The law of Moses is what makes us Jews!" cries another. "It's what separates us from the world."

"Exactly!" says Barry as he rises to his feet. "It's what separates us. But Jesus was not about separation, was he? Who is your neighbor? Is it your Brother? Your friend? A Samaritan? A Roman? Isn't that what our Master asked us?"

"Are you saying that we should throw out the laws of Moses? That our fathers were obedient for nothing?"

"No," Barry explains, "I'm not saying that at all." Then pointing to the one who asked the questions, he says, "You, Jude... You think the laws are important, yes?"

"Of course," the man says.

"And you studied them? You memorized them? You follow them?" Barry asks as if not talking to anyone in particular.

"I am a good Jew. I know the law!" the man replies adamantly.

"And you learned them all in two weeks, correct?"

"What?" the man replies shocked. "No! No one can learn the law in two weeks. It's impossible!"

"And yet," Barry retorts, "that is exactly what you are asking the Gentiles to do." There is a murmur and nodding of heads. Barry continues, "Now, there are certainly some really big ones which we can ask right away. We can make sure that they worship no other but God... that they do not eat of food offered to idols... that they keep the Sabbath... Those they can remember. The rest will come in time, but they should not have to know them all to be baptized and to come into the light."

The rest of the day is consumed with discussion of what to leave in and what to leave out. Towards the end, it is decided that it will be easier to decide what to leave out, as this is a much smaller list that most can agree upon. Barry can only laugh to himself knowing that most of this will eventually be set aside in the decades to come. Although the future theologians will argue some tough and important questions, Barry also knows the void will mostly be filled with other equally useless arguments. But the main decision is made, to the relief of the Gentiles assembled, to forgo circumcision as a requirement to be a follower of Christ.

"Score one for the Democrats!" Barry says to himself, finding himself on the opposite side of the aisle than he was in his previous life.

It is almost dark by the time Barry makes it home. Shira asks, "So, did anything big get raised?" Barry laughs as he walks into the next room. Shira looks at him perplexed and asks, "What?"

INTO THE BREACH

Barry and his family remain in Jerusalem for two more years. Shira couldn't be more pleased because it means frequent trips back to Timnah. Alon is not moving as well as he used to and Oded is doing more and more of the work. But then, Barry is not moving that well either. He feels really old when he becomes a grandfather. In the middle of the second year, Rachel gives birth to Oded's first son, Zachias. Shira spends extra time in Timnah as she helps Rachel with the birth and also plans Mary's wedding with Bracha.

Meanwhile, back at the ranch, the middle of that first year sees Ditza married as well. She was matched to a butcher's son. He is not all that good looking and is a little on the plump side, but Ditza seems to really care for him. Barry finds it harder to make this deal. She turns out to be the spitting image of Shira. Barry finds himself moping around and expecting to see her around every corner of the house. It leaves a hole in Barry's life for a while. But, he sees her often and she is very happy in her new life, so that helps a little. Barry knows she will never starve at least.

197

Shira arranges for a widow friend of hers, and sometimes Ditza, to care for Barry and Andrew while she is away in Timnah. Andrew is turning into quite the scholar and may actually follow in Barry's footsteps one day. There are days when Andrew comes from school and he and Barry sit and discuss scriptures. Andrew also loves to hear Barry's stories of Jesus and seems quite interested. Claudius is still emperor, but the northern borders are quieter now and sporadic pockets of persecution begin to resurface.

Shira has returned from Timnah, another generation now firmly in place, when a knock comes at the door. Shira opens the door and standing there is the Apostle Andrew. Shira rushes to hug him and invites him in.

"Sit," Shira commands, "and I will fix you something to eat."

"No, just something to drink is fine," Andrew says politely.

"What brings you to our home this time? If you are looking for Matthias, he and Andrew are helping out someone in town. You can wait if you wish," Shira says whisking back and forth. "How are you and your son doing since your wife passed?"

"Ok, I guess. He's married now," Andrews says, "but, I actually came to see you, Shira."

"Me?" Shira asks as a sudden stillness befalls her. Her face finds a worried look. "Why me?" she asks as she slowly places the wine on the table and sits down.

"There is a new church that is struggling to survive. It needs a man like Matthias there. It is in a large city, and if the foundation can be set, many feel that it could be a big church someday."

"Well, you know Matthias won't turn that down," Shira says with a sigh. "Where is this church?"

"Smyrna. It's on the coast, not far from Greece," Andrew explains.

"Well, it won't be the first time we've been far from home," Shira complains. But then she sees a look on Andrew's face. "But you would be telling this to Matthias," she continues. "You didn't come here to talk to me about moving."

"I won't lie to you," says Andrew, "It's dangerous. The reason the church is struggling is because the Pharisee's there are constantly stirring up trouble. There are continuous reports of persecution."

"That's never stopped him either... but you already know that too," Shira says becoming more concerned. "So why talk to me? You know he will go."

Andrew speaks in a softer voice, "When my wife died, I was so lost and you and Matthias befriended me and my son and got us though that. I love Matthias like my own brother and you as my own sister." He then starts to blush slightly and says in a sheepish voice as he reaches for her hand, "You... maybe even more so."

There is an awkward silence as they look into each other's eyes. "I'm sorry," Andrew says releasing her hand and withdrawing.

Shira, a little flustered, says, "No... It's alright Andrew. I understand. I'm touched."

"I don't wish to see either of you harmed," Andrew continues. "If you wish it, I will not ask Matthias to go. I will give an excuse to the others."

"Funny," Shira says in contemplation. "If you had told me this when we first began this crazy life together, I would have forbidden you to ask him. I didn't understand Jesus then. But Matthias and I are both here today because of a man who wouldn't say 'no' to us. I now find that I too have as hard a time saying 'no' to him as Matthias does.

We will go." They both stand and Shira moves to kiss Andrew on the cheek. "You don't have to tell him," she says. "I will."

"I will tell the others. I will pray to see you both again."

"May God's blessing go with you, Andrew," Shira says as she opens the door.

"And with you," Andrew says on the way out the door.

Later in the day, Barry and son Andrew return. Shira meets them in the front room. She hugs and kisses Barry.

"Why are you two always kissing?" Andrew asks. "My friend's parents don't kiss all the time."

"That you see..." says Barry. "Your mother and I don't kiss in public."

"And we kiss," Shira says, "because we love each other so much. One day I hope that you will have a wife that you can love that much."

"Yuck," Andrew says waving his hand, "I can wait..."

"You say that now," Shira replies. She shoos him away saying, "Go clean up for supper."

Shira then relates to Barry all the things Andrew had conveyed. "I told him we would go."

"That's a long way, Shira. And I worry about taking you someplace like that. Are you sure you want to go?" Barry asks.

"No. But, my place is with you. I'm not afraid anymore. But I do worry about Andrew."

"And I know he would miss school. He's old enough to leave with Oded, isn't he?"

"Rachel is busy with the baby. I'll send word to Bracha. They both can watch him."

As Andrew returns, Shira asks, "Papa and I have to go on a long trip, would you like to stay with your Aunt Bracha and play with James?"

"Yeah!" Andrew cheers.

"Well, I guess that's settled," Barry chuckles.

Barry loads up his small wagon with things they will need for the church. Barry also has to trade for another donkey. Barry isn't sure how old Ruffy is, but traders put him somewhere between twenty-five and thirty years old. He is a world traveler and has been a faithful worker. But Barry isn't sure that Ruffy has one more long trip left in him. So he thanks Ruffy for his long service, especially the one trip that saved Shira's life. He trades for a five year old donkey that he officially names 'Ruffy II', but just calls Ruffy when nobody's listening.

After dropping off Andrew in Timnah, Shira and Barry head out into the unknown once again. It is late in the morning and the sun beats down on the small wagon. They are between the last village and the next village in the middle of nowhere. The road is dry and dusty and the miles trudge by undiscernibly. As Barry thinks he might nod off any time, he hears a noise in the distance.

"What is that noise? Thunder?" Barry asks as he scans the sky. "I don't see any clouds."

"There," Shira says as she points to the horizon ahead of them. Barry sees a giant cloud of dust rising. "Can that be the wind?" asks Shira puzzled.

"That's no wind," Barry mutters. "That's riders on horses. They're headed this way, and if the cloud is any indication, there are more than a few of them and they're riding hard."

""Maybe we should pull off the road and try to hide."

"There is no place to hide. Besides, if we do that we make ourselves look suspicious."

"What do we do? What if they find the church things?"

"Relax," Barry says in a reassuring tone, "there is no way anybody would know we would be on this road today. They'll probably just ride right by."

Shira is more skeptical. The cloud swells and the noise becomes louder. Barry can now see the tops of the riders as they crest the hill. There are eight riders and they are all lightly armored and must be part of a local militia. As they approach, they begin to slow their pace. Barry begins to think to himself, "Dang it. I *hate* it when Shira is right. Maybe we should have tried to get off the road." They stop ahead of Barry and force him to stop the wagon.

"What is your business on this road?" barks one of the men.

"We are from Timnah. On a trip to visit family," Barry says.

"Search the wagon," demands the man. Three of men dismount and go to the back of the wagon.

"What are you looking for?" asks Barry.

"Shut your mouth," the man barks. The men begin to take stuff off the wagon in a hurried fashion and throw it to the ground.

"Hey, be careful with that," Barry demands as he stands and watches them closely.

"I told you to shut up," the man in charge barks again as a couple of the men who remain mounted draw their weapons. Barry sits back down but continues to watch the men. Very quickly, the men by the wagon have thrown several things to the ground and one says, "There's no one here, sir."

"Mount up," the man in charge commands. The men quickly spring back onto their horses and the entire group thunders away, leaving Barry hacking in a thick cloud of dust.

"Who were they looking for?" asks Shira.

"I don't know," Barry says climbing down off the wagon, "but it wasn't us." He walks towards the back of the wagon and yells in the direction that the men exited, "Next time bring a warrant!"

"A what?" Shira asks?

Barry chuckles, "Never mind. It doesn't matter."

As Barry reloads the wagon, he examines each item for damage before replacing it in its place. It is once again a reminder that he lives under occupation where the ruling class can do whatever they wish. And he and Shira are headed into the lion's mouth. This trip is not starting out very well. Barry hopes it is not an omen. After he finishes reloading the wagon, he climbs up and they continue on their journey, none the worse for wear - this time.

After a long journey, Barry and Shira arrive at Smyrna, a large Hellenistic port city on the mouth of the Hermus River. Barry is leading the donkey and Shira sits in the wagon as the streets become busier the further in they go. They are both taken by the beauty of the city as it rises up the adjacent mountain like tiers on a wedding cake. The streets are broad and well paved. They crisscross at right angles. Barry whispers to himself, "Now this is more like Manhattan... without the cars..." Many of the streets are named after the temple that resides on them. The main street, called 'Golden', is bustling with people of all races, some that Barry has never seen since he arrived through the portal.

As Barry leads through the marketplaces, he inquires in a very general way trying to find a starting place for his search in this sea of humanity. If the persecution is as frequent as rumored, then Barry must be careful as the church will be mostly 'underground' and strangers will be looked upon with suspicion. After a successive string of persons to talk to, Barry receives the name of a merchant who may belong to the church. After navigating the maze of streets and congestion, Barry and Shira walk into a fabric shop. A small Turkish man folds a piece of linen by a table.

"You are Fakir?" Barry asks.

"Yes, welcome to my shop, my friend," he replies. Turning to Shira he asks, "What are you looking for today?"

Shira's eyes get big and she says, "Oh, these fabrics are so beautiful..." She moves to one of the tables.

"Of course!" exclaims Fakir. "The best fabric in all the region! And yet, brought to you at the best prices, of course."

"Look at this one, Matthias," Shira says holding it up to look at fully.

"Matthias? That is a Hebrew name, no?" Fakir asks quizzically.

"Yes. We are from a town near to Jerusalem," replies Barry.

"Ah, I don't get many people here from Jerusalem. It's a long way to come to purchase cloth. What brings you here?" Fakir asks cautiously.

"We have family in the area but have never seen the city. So, we're just looking around," Barry says calmly.

"I've never seen this color," Shira says as she becomes lost in perusing the merchandise.

"That one comes all the way from the far east of Asia Minor," Fakir replies as he keeps one eye on Barry.

"The city is larger than I thought it would be..." Barry continues.

"Yes, very large," Fakir says.

"There's probably many gods worshiped here..." Barry muses.

"Yes, yes. Many temples."

"We will need to find a place to worship while in town. Can you help us with that?"

"Me? And what advice would a good Pharisee seek from a simple Turk, such as myself? I think there is a synagogue on the west end of town," Fakir says.

"I was actually looking for someone who could help me find a man who died on a tree."

"A man of bread?..." Fakir asks.

"And of wine," Barry responds.

"Who are you?" Fakir demands.

"I am the Apostle Matthias, one of the twelve. I've come to help you with the church," Barry explains.

A great sigh of relief comes over Fakir. "I was afraid you were a Pharisee. Come, quickly," he says as he motions them to the back room. Barry grabs Shira's arm as she is still lost in looking and pulls her towards the room. Fakir tells his wife to watch the shop and she goes out as Fakir closes the door.

"We must be very careful," Fakir says. "The Pharisees hate us and meddle in everything we do, setting the local authorities against us."

"Pharisees from Jerusalem?" Barry asks.

"No. They are locals."

"Good," Barry sighs, "then they are less likely to know me."

"Come back before sunset, and I will take you to where some of us meet. You will eat with us, yes?"

"God's blessings upon your house," Barry says as they walk back out into the front of the shop.

They exit the shop and wander the city for the rest of the day, taking in its beauty and diversity. Shira is continually amazed at all the sights and sounds. It is much different than Ethiopia, but still wondrous. Barry and Shira arrive back at Fakir's about half an hour before sunset. He takes them out of the main city into the lower city. The streets here are similar, but are always damp and littered with puddles and mud because of the closeness to the shore and bad drainage. They soon arrive at a small house and are welcomed in. Five families crowd together in this small house as they break bread together and bask in the warm fellowship. Fakir introduces Barry to the group and there is a general consensus that thing are looking up, now that they have a 'real apostle'. Barry tells them stories of Jesus and corrects others that have been told with errors. One of the families agrees to allow Barry and Shira to stay with them. Sadik and his wife have no children living with them and so they have an extra room. Shira is once more thrown into a tailspin as she has to set aside most of her Jewish customs, this time to assume the life of a Turkish Gentile. Barry takes it all in stride.

Barry is able to bring some form of order to the church. He brings a consistency that they had been missing to the teachings and stories. The scrolls and other articles he brought with him help stabilize the church and eliminate most of the arguments and debates. As a result, the church begins to grow exponentially. It's all Barry can do to keep up, as he sends reports back to Jerusalem and asks for them to send help. Although the church is growing large, many of the members are not leaders and their faith is very shallow. It is continually tested as the Pharisees detain them in search of more names and meeting locations. At one point, Barry asks Shira to leave and retreat to a place where it is safer, but Shira refuses. But even with all the difficulties and threats, the Word of God is unstoppable in this city.

For almost two years, the church grows, though not as fast as it did in the beginning. Barry manages to stay one step ahead of the Pharisees and he is unofficially growing in power, as the prefect for this region knows Barry has the ear of a large portion of the population. The Pharisees see no choice to protect their own power base but to take drastic action. They convince the prefect to arrest Barry and put him into prison. The prefect is hesitant as he is afraid riots will break out, but he eventually gives in after extracting heavy concessions from the Pharisees.

Barry finds himself in a prison cell of stone. He has a heavy, rusty chain that binds his right ankle to the wall. It is damp and poorly lit. He has only a stone slab to sit and sleep on. He is fed a small bowl of soup once a day. There are no windows, so it is hard to tell the day from the night and time tends to just slip away as days turn into weeks. Shira is allowed to visit him on a weekly basis. She tells him of how the church split. Some have run away into hiding after his arrest, but the others are now stronger and more determined. Shira takes over running the church for her part. Barry is in some ways surprised, but in other ways not. She tells him stories of successes to try and bolster his spirit, as his health is greatly deteriorating.

One day a figure of a man appears at the door to his cell. Barry strains to see who it is. "Oded?" Barry asks weakly.

"Papa. I have come."

"Why?"

"I am going to talk to the prefect tomorrow. I'm going to get you released so we can go home." Oded says confidently.

"I can't go home," Barry says with a cough. "Take your mother and go."

"I have to try, papa." Oded says with a strain in his voice.

"Try then. But do not give in to false hope."

"Why has God abandoned you here?"

"Abandon?" Barry asks with a bit of renewed strength. "No, not abandoned. He is using me, even now."

"I don't understand."

"I know. But learn from your mother and someday you shall."

"Is there anything I can get you?"

Barry contemplates for a second and then says, "Quill and scroll, if you can."

"I love you, papa. I will get you out of here." Oded says as the guard begins to shove him away.

"And I, you. God's blessings upon you." Barry's voice trails off.

Some time later, a guard returns and opens the door. He drops a piece of parchment and a crude piece of a charcoal-like stone on the ground at Barry's feet and Barry says, "Thank you." He then leaves without a word and closes the door. Barry picks up the items, sits on the ground next to the stone slab and uses the slab as a writing surface and to sharpen the writing stone. His hands shake in his weakened condition and the light is so poor, it is hard to see what he is writing. But the writing seems to lend purpose to his time, even if only momentarily. And once he begins, he writes with fervor to record his thoughts as he tries to sum up his life as best he can.

He writes lots of instructions to the church and to specific people and then concludes with, "This will be the last gospel of Matthias. What can I say of my life? I am far from where I started, and so close to where I'm going now. It was not the direction I intended to go, but it was the path I needed to walk. I have nothing of what I started out wanting, but now have everything that I need and that I now want. God has brought me to this place to serve his need and his purpose. I have nothing of my own, but all that God has, he has given to me. Even now, I give thanks for the love and hope and peace that surround me now and in the time to come."

"And what of my works? There have been many, but of what worth are they to me now? For who in prison can boast, 'see me and what I have done!' and be believed? I have done nothing. If I have brought someone into the light of God, then surely it was the Spirit's working in them and God deserves the glory. If I have caused my brother to fall, then the shame is mine alone. When I stand in judgment, shall I say to the Lord, 'Look, here are all the souls I saved.'? No, for it is not in my power to save a soul. Shall I say, 'Here is a list of all of the things I've done for you.'? No, for the Lord will show me the list of all of the things that went undone from my sin. When I stand before the Lord, I shall say, 'Lord, I did as you asked but so often I failed. I went where you have sent me but always with complaints. I have tried to follow in your son's example the best that I knew how, but always fell short.' And the Lord, who never stopped loving me, will tell me that I am forgiven because his Son has already paid the price for me. For in the end, when all is said and done, when all of our works and deeds and intentions and victories are split asunder, the only soul we can truly save is our own. That is the only true task that God has called each of us to."

"To those who come after me, love the Lord. Do not expect him when you want him, but expect him when you need him. Do all in your power to honor his majesty and he will lead you to Eden."

A few days later, a detail of soldiers shows up outside his cell. The regular guard opens the door and removes the shackle from Barry's ankle. Barry hands the rolled parchment to the guard.

"I do not know your name, but you have never shown ill will towards me. Give this to my son, please?" Barry pleads.

"I do not know why you are here. You have always thanked me for just doing my duty and nothing more. For you, I will make this effort," the guard replies.

The soldiers lead Barry out of the prison. They lead him a short distance to an open field where empty wood crosses loosely litter the space like spread fingers on uplifted hands. The detail stops next to where workers take one of the crosses and lay it down. They put Barry down and begin to bind him to the cross. When that is accomplished, the group strain to raise the cross and it drops back into its hole with a dreadful thud. The detail leaves and Barry hangs in the beating sun.

People walk past and give some notice as Barry starts to grow weary and passes in and out of consciences. Barry sees people from the church walk past. Some of them stop and stare. Some shed tears while others look in disdain as if disappointed with the results. Some cannot make eye contact at all as the shame yokes them and makes it hard for them to even lift their heads as they walk away. Shira and Oded appear near the foot of the cross as Barry struggles to open his eyes. Oded has the scroll. There are some that stop to console Shira. Barry can see the tears streaming down the face that he remembers so radiant as they stood under the marriage tent and kissed for the first time as husband and wife.

"Do not cry, my wife," Barry struggles to say to Shira through labored breathing. "I want to remember only your smile. I go to the place you know and I will wait for you. This goodbye is not forever."

"I will not waiver," Shira replies, "For your Master is my Master and I will serve him as you did."

Then Barry looks to Oded and says, "Take care of your mother, son. Take that scroll to Jerusalem and put it into James' hand. Learn from them."

"It will be done as you ask," says Oded.

Barry's breathing is extremely labored. The time is close and he approaches the gate. It is of smooth, white stone and is lit up by the sun reflecting of the polished surface. The door is of golden bars and it swings open. There is a bright light all around and Barry uses his last remaining effort to look up. He sees Jesus standing in the gate with open arms. "It's time to come home... 'Ya did good!'" Jesus says to him. No more proof does Barry require.

ABOUT THE AUTHOR

Dave Dillon was born in Ft Worth and has been a Texan all his life, spending the vast majority of his time on this Earth in the Dallas area. He currently resides close to Austin.
He is both a computer geek and a Pastor in the United Methodist Church. He loves science fiction, history and theology and all topics of discussion where they overlap.

Made in the USA
Columbia, SC
20 February 2023